GIRL ON HEAVEN'S PIER

T0247479

Eeva-Liisa Manner

Girl on Heaven's Pier

A NOVEL

Translated by Terhi Kuusisto

DALKEY ARCHIVE PRESS

Originally published in Finnish as *Tytto taivaan laiturilla* by Werner Söderström Osakeyhtiö in 1951.

Library of Congress Cataloging-in-Publication Data
Names: Manner, Eeva-Liisa, author. | Kuusisto, Terhi, translator.
Title: Girl on heaven's pier / Eeva-Liisa Manner ; translated by Terhi
  Kuusisto.
Other titles: Tytto taivaan laiturilla. English
Description: First Dalkey Archive edition. | Victoria, TX : Dalkey Archive
  Press, 2016. | Originally published in Finnish as Tytto taivaan laiturilla
  by W. Sèoderstrèom (Porvoo, 1951).
Identifiers: LCCN 2016010762 | ISBN 9781628971385 (pbk. : alk. paper)
Subjects: LCSH: Girls--Fiction. | Grandparent and child--Fiction. |
  Perception in children--Fiction. | Reality--Fiction. | Vyborg
  (Russia)--Fiction. | Psychological fiction.
Classification: LCC PH355.M25 T9813 2016 | DDC 894/.54133--dc23
LC record available at https://lccn.loc.gov/2016010762

FILI FINNISH LITERATURE EXCHANGE

Partially funded by a grant by the Illinois Arts Council, a state agency. This work has been published with the financial assistance of FILI– Finnish Literature Exchange

www.dalkeyarchive.com
Victoria, TX / McLean, IL / Dublin

Dalkey Archive Press publications are, in part, made possible through the support of the University of Houston-Victoria and its programs in creative writing, publishing, and translation.

Cover: Art by Katherine O'Shea
Printed on permanent/durable acid-free paper

Over carnations, roses, lilies,
She picked a stinging nettle,
That's all I know.
So goes the tale
That alone will tell what veil
Wears the white bird of fairy tale.
                    —Aale Tynni

ONCE UPON A TIME, not far from here, not long ago, there was a bit of geometry that had become wood and stone—a town that no longer exists. Or if it does, it's no longer real or accessible to us—it lives only in the past, has indeed become the past. Perhaps because of just that, it is more beautiful than real towns; real towns are dreams turned into reality, our town is reality turned into a dream. It's perfect because it has ceased to exist; it's eternal because it is dead.

In many ways this town was different from others even in its lifetime. It was an extremely honorable town, it had History, but it did not, however, worry too much about its dignity. It knew how to laugh. Besides, the passing human notion of time had oddly stopped on its streets. It almost felt like there was no time at all. The old and the new, today and yesterday, were mingled and tangled, mixed up and sorted in this town, and each seemed to bask in the other's company. If lucky, you could find wormwood or sorrel in the middle of the street, sustaining its wretched life between the tram track and a cobblestone. And like yellow sardine tins, the trams rattled on in the midst of the ancient houses that were nicely weathered, tilted in a melancholy way, but the elderly houses didn't mind, despite their ageless gloom. In some other place such noisy, mechanical progress might not have been considered seemly and worthy of decadent finery, but in our town it was fondly tolerated, even found appropriate.

It was also appropriate that near the town center, where the streets and houses and squares had been neatly drawn using a compass and ruler, there was a thoroughly ugly brick building, a house of correction for little boys and girls, an elementary school. In this house, two-hundred human seedlings were raised and corrected, here they broke the law and tried to get ahead; among the others, in her thick cotton frock, there was Leena, who had come from a tilted wooden house on the edge of town—where you could find sorrel between cobblestone and rail, if lucky.

"MARCH TO THE RHYTHM—one two, one two . . ."

The teacher was standing at the end of the line, clapping her hands together and counting. In this school everything had to happen in beautiful order.

Leena's feet lifted grudgingly, and grudgingly she watched the swinging plaits of the girl in front of her. Then her eyes turned to look at the stone floor, which was black and bare like a sauna's floor. Here it also echoed like in the sauna where she and Grandma bathed on Saturdays. The teacher's voice was frighteningly strict and almost angry when she was counting out the beat for the girls. Then she commanded:

"You may enter the classroom now—in you go."

The line obeyed. Like little soldiers with skirts on, the girls stepped into the classroom, split into four smaller lines, and found their desks.

"Sit."

The teacher sat down herself and started to make marks

in a journal. Leena's eyes wandered around blotchy maroon walls, her lips silently moving. Why couldn't they have painted the walls something more beautiful, say the color of oranges. Everything was so thoroughly ugly and dirty, dirty-looking at least. And the windows were quite naked, so that looking at them made you cold. Why couldn't they hang some curtains, bright, with pretty colors, curtains with flowers and birds and funny miniature houses. Or cats and angels. Although it had to be up to the teachers. Maybe they didn't like beautiful colors. At least their teacher didn't. Their teacher was even now dressed in an ugly brown dress with small grayish-yellow dots. The dots where quite especially ugly, but for some reason it was impossible not to stare at them, and she stared at them so that eventually the whole world was filled with hateful dirty-yellow dots that kept going round and round and filled her head with their buzzing. Sometimes she would try to count the dots of the teacher's dress but she always got mixed-up before she could finish. And then she thought that there was no end to them, and the thought was so terrifying it made her dizzy. Those dots made her afraid of the teacher, too. Or not really, it wasn't the dots. The teacher was not a real person, somehow she was half-thing, a thing or . . . an institution that one had to be afraid of. *Had* to be afraid, it was a rule and command that could not be broken. And then the teacher never laughed, and that just added to her thingness. Things can't laugh, nor could the teacher. If only, just once, she'd said something playful, even by mistake, Leena might have forgiven her for those ugly dots, too. But the teacher was solidly solemn, solemn like . . . yes, like a hymn. Leena disliked hymns, for Grandma sang hymns all the time, and they were solemn enough to make you cry, and always about sin. And Leena began to wonder whether she'd perhaps been put in this ugly school for some strange sin, but she couldn't remember her sins, and thus felt bitter disappointment. If she had just one nice sin to ponder piously and religiously and repent properly, she might have better tolerated the school. But since not even sin gave her consolation, she was left puzzled and gave in to shattering terror.

And she gave in to her terror with all her heart, like it was her only hobby. She couldn't help being horrified by the school, being as horrified as could be by the teacher—just like she was horrified by all the people who had no smile. The teacher had no smile, instead she had a beard. When Leena first saw the thin whiskers growing on the teacher's chin, it had given her a terrible fright, and after this discovery she felt the teacher was even less human than before.

"Leena!"

Leena got up, frightened. She understood that the

teacher had asked her something, but she hadn't heard the question.

"Well?"

Leena stared at the dirty-yellow dots that in her eyes started moving around in a large circle.

"Have you been daydreaming again? Sit down and write—listen carefully now—'Martti is a proper name and is capitalized.' Write it in ink, ten times. But watch yourself so that don't stain the desk! The desks are brand new, and they have cost the school a lot of money."

Leena sat down. She felt a great weariness, and at the same time she was afraid. The teacher had warned her about the desk again. The desk really was brand new, very nice and extraordinarily shiny—the only thing at their school that was nice and shiny. Slowly she got out her writing things. Unscrewing the ink bottle she prayed fervently to God to not let the ink bottle fall and ruin the desk—and then it happened. She didn't understand how it happened, in a dreamlike state she just saw the ink running across the desktop, dripping onto the floor. And it felt like she had fallen into cold water, and through the water she could hear the blurred, distant sound of the teacher's angry voice. And when she awoke, she was standing in the corner by the vestibule and she could feel her palms sweating. And facing her was the maroon wall, and on the wall a shapeless stain, a ghastly ghost looking at her with its one eye and then slowly spreading its mouth into an awful smile.

Leena closed her eyes and tried to think. She felt the eyes of her peers on the back of her neck, and she felt like they were at least a hundred. She was afraid of her peers, too—afraid of all of them together, but none of them separately. The teacher had to be feared separately. And this shame . . . She wasn't saddened about the desk, or the damage—in fact it served the desk right for being so infuriatingly nice and clean and having to be looked after, like it was the finest thing in the whole world.

"Shit."

She didn't say it out loud—she would never have dared—but she muttered it very solemnly and seriously and it comforted her enormously.

The feeling of comfort was followed by tears that rose up her throat, and she felt that she'd been wronged. She had prayed to God not to let the bottle fall, and God had failed her. Or who knows . . . who knows if God is even . . .

She didn't have time to finish the thought before the bell rang and the class started to hum.

"Quiet, quiet please . . . Get in line! One two, one two . . . Leena stays."

The teacher lowered her voice when she said the last words, but Leena pretended not to hear, just stood dumbly in the corner, not turning her head.

The steel tip of the teacher's pen rustled on paper.

"You may take this note to your parents. Well, come on, now."

Slowly Leena emerged from her nook and stood in front of the lectern. Her chin did not reach the edge of the teacher's desk.

"Give this to your mother, Leena. I want to have a talk with her."

Leena's fingers grabbed the paper reluctantly.

"I have no mother," she mumbled defiantly.

"What's that? Oh . . . Well, give it to Father, then." The teacher coughed. "You do have a father?"

Leena did not utter a word. She stared intensely at the hollow pen holder so that she wouldn't have to see the dots and the beard.

"Come now, Leena, what does your father do," the teacher pleaded with her.

"Father . . . I don't know. Grandma says he drinks."

The teacher's face had reddened, and she bit her lip. Leena felt that she needed to explain further.

"He's abroad and married. Grandma says he married again, and drinks. And he plays with a piano at a restaurant."

"Plays the piano," corrected the teacher. "There, you do know."

"Yes, but not for sure. Grandma says you never know, he might be dead."

"Your father?"

"Yes."

"You've never seen him?"

Leena shook her head. The teacher wasn't using her normal school voice anymore, and so she found the courage to say: "But I have an uncle. He's a Second Lieutenant."

It came out like she had said, "My uncle is a General."

"Is that so," the teacher said. "And you live with him?"

"No, with Grandma. My uncle is far away, flying. He's a flying second lieutenant."

"A-ha." The teacher was playing with the ruler. Then she said, "How old are you?"

"Nine years old."

"Well, then. You are such a big girl, now, you should be a much better pupil. Second-graders are usually eight."

Leena realized she had to defend herself.

"But I was sick," she said miserably.

"Indeed. I think I remember it now. You had scarlet fever and that's why you couldn't start school on time, correct?"

"Yes."

"And you started directly in the second grade?"

"Yes."

"Who taught you to read and write?"

"Nobody taught . . ."

"Did you teach yourself?"

"Yes."

"That's just it. They should have put you in the first

grade. You can't follow the lessons. Well, we shall think about it. Take that note to your grandmother now, Leena. You may go."

LEENA WANDERED OUT of the classroom slowly, crossed the hall floor that resembled a sauna floor, idled sleepily down the stairs, her shoulder dragging along the wall, and stopped on the landing by the window. Without a thought she stared out the window, fingered the paper the teacher had given her, and bent its corners into dog ears, then spread it out in front of her and started to make out the words:

To Leena's parents:

Unfortunately I must let you know that Leena is a worryingly lazy and stubborn pupil. I hope that you will be kind enough to come by the school someday so that we can discuss Leena's upbringing in some detail.

Ida Nieminen, Leena's teacher

At that moment Leena heard the classroom door closing and someone approaching the stairs. It's the teacher, she thought with concern, and shoved the letter into her apron pocket. Then she pretended to blow her nose and waited. With some difficulty, panting a little, the teacher descended the steep stairs and went past her without a word. She puffs out hate, thought Leena, pressing herself closer to the window. And she felt some shapeless mean feeling gaining force and gathering in her throat. It wasn't shame, it was hate. But as soon as the teacher had gone and the footsteps had given way to silence in the dark corridor, the hate faded and dispersed into vague sadness. It was an oddly powerless, yet infinite sorrow, it was all over her, and she felt that nothing, nothing could take it away from her. It was an endlessly long, eternal sorrow, sorrow that couldn't be explained, yet was quite obvious. And it wasn't because of the teacher and that miserable piece of paper, now she just *remembered* it clearer than usual. Remembered, yes—for it had always existed in and around her, even if it could sometimes be forgotten. It was a sorrow that contained all that she knew or understood: a tree, a bird, sky, cloud, rain, wind, people. Rain, yes. Rain crying against the window, and something crying inside of her. Rain . . . It was a beautiful word, and sorrow . . . Beautiful, too. Rainsorrow—sorrowrain—this is how she makes up beautiful new words.

And suddenly she felt that the sorrow had gained a

gentle glow. She pressed her cheek against the window, and it felt like the pane was shivering softly. The pane felt longing, the pane was cold and it yearned as the rain cried relentlessly against it. Just like that, something was crying inside her, too—relentlessly, constantly, evenly, silently. Like the rain. What was it crying for, that rain? Maybe it was crying for the same reason as her. Why she cried, she did not know, and that made everything feel so sad. House, sky, rain, tree, clouds . . . as if everything had been put into this sorrow. Along with her of course, Leena. That she had been put there—that everything was ready, and nothing could be changed—that had to be where this universal sorrow came from.

Then Leena noticed that her cheek was wet, and she no longer knew if it was raining outside or inside the windowpane. The rain trickled slowly down her cheek, and it started to feel strangely good to her—sad and meaningless and good. Everything drowned in the rain, and she thought that if she stood in the rain like this for long enough, she herself would turn into rain, all of her, and the sadness too, would turn into rain, which was like a monotonous song, indifferent, lulling, almost silent.

"Hey you! Outside—be quick now! No loitering in the hallway during recess. Put on your jacket and go out and play!"

It was the principal's voice—impossibly loud and

vigorous and almost happy. The principal was always like that. Standing on the upper landing like a revelation, turning the wide, square back towards her, to disappear into the corridor.

Leena was hurt, not exactly by the principal, but somehow in general. The sorrow was ruined, her very own sorrow that the rain had made beautiful and turned into a song. She pushed her hair out of her face, blew her nose and crept down the stairs into the hall where the coats were kept in ugly, awkward racks that looked like gallows. Every morning the coats were hanged. Every morning. Every morning—something—hanged.

Leena didn't develop the thought any further, if it was a thought at all—more just something like a blurry image. Hurriedly she snatched her coat and cap off the rack, rushed into the yard and kept going, out the gate. The school rules strictly prohibited going into the street during recess, but she didn't care about that now. She had a liberating, yet melancholy feeling that the rules no longer applied to her.

When she reached the street corner, the bell gave a rattling ring and the noisy children ran to line up. Leena put her coat on slowly and listened indifferently to the roar that was dying out in the yard as one line after another marched in. It sounded strange and distant. She knew she had once marched in line, but that was very long ago. So long ago she couldn't even recall their teacher. She remembered only the dots . . .

No, she wouldn't go to school anymore.

But she wouldn't go home, either, because she wanted to be alone, alone with the rain and her sorrow. She still wanted to get away from here, away from the ugly school. She'd go to the river, to look at the water and listen to the music the water made.

IT WASN'T REALLY A RIVER—she was just exaggerating. It was part of the great sea, a bay or inlet or something like that; it flowed slowly under the bridge on the edge of town, and that's why she called it a river.

Leena had always loved water and been afraid of it at the same time. There was something terrible about water, and yet it mysteriously attracted her. And underwater there was another odd, beautiful world, the watery garden.

When she looked into the water to see her reflection shimmering on the surface, the piece of paper given to her by the teacher rustled in her pocket, and the spell was broken. Leena stuck her tongue out at her reflection and opened the note to spell out the message once more. This time it could not make an impression on her, though—the words felt oddly meaningless and dull, like they were about somebody else, and not about her at all. And suddenly it was clear that the paper wanted to fly—to turn into a bird and fly. So she folded the paper once, pressed the corners together and folded once again, and there was the bird. Before she had time for reflection, it bravely took flight, paused for a second in midair, and then slowly and gracefully slid onto the water's surface. In the water it spread its wings and tried to rise into the air one more time but could not—or maybe it didn't want to. The bird loved water like her, and the water carried it far away, as far as the eye could see, and further. All the way to foreign lands.

Leena felt a longing. Not really for the bird or even for foreign lands, but for something she couldn't explain. The bird had to go, it was a migrating bird, and it was autumn, and the water was cold. But somehow she longed for the *going*. She felt such longing every time someone left. And yet everybody went—summer, autumn, warmth, the bird—only she was left. Left behind. Someone forgot . . . forgot to take her.

She felt like getting really sad and blue, but then she remembered the water. Water, too, was always flowing away, yet not really leaving. It was indestructible and eternal like the sky or God. God, yes—for Leena felt that water saw everything and knew everything. Water could tell everything like a mirror or window, just in much more mysterious and exciting ways. Everything that happened onshore also happened underwater, yet upside-down. Houses were upside-down in the water, trees stood on their heads in the water, the water turned everything bottom up. But all things looked more beautiful turned upside down than normally, water gave everything a wonderful glimmer. Or who knows—maybe the water told tales . . . Leena knew the water could tell tales. Water showed many things in the wrong light. An ordinary stone could look very special in water, it could wear a transparent dress, or it could be like some strange being, a silver mouse or cat. But when you picked up the stone and lifted it out of the water, the glimmer disappeared, the shine was gone. The stone lost its pretty dress and was ugly and wet and slimy, just a regular stone. Water lied, Leena thought.

But when she started thinking about it more carefully, she couldn't be absolutely sure. What if the water was right—what if *she saw it wrong* as soon as she lifted the beautiful wet stone out of the water. Or maybe she saw it for real but the shore was jealous and ripped the stone of its beautiful dress. Yes, the thought was a very complicated one, and she couldn't make sense of it. But she was quite sure that if she was a fish or stone or flower underwater, she would see all of the water things in the right way. Then she'd know. If she decided to go and live underwater she would know.

If she went underwater . . . But she couldn't live underwater. How might it feel to die in the water?—And suddenly she knew. She knew it like she had once died in water.

She was watching the clouds sliding down the river, and suddenly it felt like she began to slide with them. Then everything began to tilt slowly, everything turned upside down, and a white light, awfully bright, lit up somewhere. And the sky was underneath her, she swam in the sky, she had wings, and everything else had dispersed. There was no earth, just the sky and the wings and that wonderful light.

Then the light dimmed, everything turned around again, the sky darkened, and through the darkness you could hear a hollow music, muted, like it was coming from underground. It was the current.

SHE SLOWLY ROSE OUT of somewhere very deep and dark to a faded dusk, and the rising scared her and made her feel a strange and awful pain, and she would rather have sunk back into darkness. But she had to come up, whether she wanted to or not, because something strong and mysterious, wind or current, had seized her and was pushing her towards the shore and the light. She knew that she was dead and that God had sent the wind or current for her, and hence she was afraid. But the further she ascended, the more trusting her mind became, and the dusk brightened around her and its reddish hue filtered through her eyelids. And when she opened her eyes a little, she saw trees and flowers and beautiful birds on every branch. And the flowers oozed a heady fragrance and the birds sang heavenly melodies, and suddenly she realized they were singing *her* songs, songs that she had made up. At that moment she realized she was in Heaven.

But the more intensely she listened, the fainter the

birdsong became, with the tune fading and escaping from her. And then she suddenly saw that the birds had been painted on the wall, and they sang no more. And the flowers were pictures, too, and they had lost all their fragrance. And so she understood she was looking at the wallpaper she had often looked at before, though she couldn't remember where. And she heard a low murmur of voices, but didn't know where the voices came from and what they meant. She only knew that she wasn't in Heaven; surely there were no such colorful wallpapers on Heaven's walls, and they were a little shabby, too. Nevertheless, she had *almost* been to Heaven, since the wallpaper had smelled nice and had been singing, singing her own songs.

She squeezed her eyes tightly shut and wished for the return of Heaven and the songs. But there was no miracle; instead she began to hear the ordinary human voices more and more clearly.

And then she felt that someone was sitting on the edge of her bed, holding her hand; the hand was big and warm and safe, and it felt nice to rest her hand in it. She opened her eyes and looked, and a strange man in a white robe was sitting by her side.

It's Jesus, Leena thought, pleased.

Or is it—the man's so fat. In pictures Jesus was always lean and had a beard. But Leena liked to think that the robed stranger was Jesus, and she figured that Jesus had shaven his beard and eaten a lot of buns in Heaven.

"I'm not dead?" she asked Jesus in astonishment.

Jesus's friendly, fat face smiled, and in a calm voice he said:

"No, you have only dreamed. Try to get some more sleep."

Leena took his advice. It felt good to obey that calm, nice voice, so she closed her eyes and obediently went back to sleep, and her hand fell asleep in the robed man's hand.

When she opened her eyes again her hand rested on the quilt all alone and she was looking at Grandma's face, an old, small, wrinkled face, sunken to almost nothing. Grandma was almost immaterial herself—like a paper cutting that you could lift against the light and see through.

"Did he go, Jesus?"

"What do you—what Jesus?"

"The Bun Jesus? With the robe . . .?"

"Robe? That was the doctor. He's gone."

"Doctor? Why?"

"Because you're sick."

Grandma's voice was dry and feeble and it rustled like paper. However, she looked like she wanted to cry if she only could. Grandma couldn't cry. Leena knew that Grandma had cried out all her tears after her second son ran away to sea and fell over the railing, drunk. Looking at Grandma, Leena felt a dutiful need to comfort, to say that Uncle Matti had surely found the drunken fall over the railing exciting, and drowning was nothing to cry about, she knew that from experience. But she was immensely tired, and words were very complicated and almost useless when you had to concoct an explanation that was appealing and also seemed true. So she just said: "Don't worry. You shouldn't worry."

"Yes I should, about such an awful sickness. He said, the doctor said you have . . . wait, I wrote it down . . . ep-i-lep-sy, it says here. That's it, ep-i-lep-sy."

"Ep-i-lep-sy." Leena tilted her head to listen. "How fun. Almost like Leena la-la lep-py-pep-py-lip-sis. What does that mean, guess! That Leena la-la—"

"Stop singing. It means a falling sickness."

"Why?"

"Because you're such an odd girl, that's why. The manor's man found you on Papulahti beach, unconscious, and carried you home. You were lying like a stone, all lifeless and with your eyes rolled back in your head. Eyes rolled back like you were possessed, said the man. And then he fetched the doctor. Though that doctor, he knew nothing, all he said was, 'Let's wait and see. And time will tell whether it's the falling sickness or something else.'"

"Like what?" asked Leena, looking precocious.

"Hard to remember everything he said. He was saying it could be hysteria, but that's pure madness, absolute crazy talk. Too much knowledge can confuse anyone, and this doctor of yours was too wise for his own good. Hysterical, I'll say . . ."

"What does it matter—if I have hyst . . . fallen sickness, I mean?"

"We'll see what it matters. It's expensive, that much I know. These modern diseases sure cost a lot. Why, valerian and Devil's dung aren't good enough to heal people anymore. I haven't needed any other drops, though, and I've lived to an old age and been fairly well." Grandma's concern seemed to lessen as she ranted, and she continued from all her heart: "To be burdened by luxury diseases, too, like Godless people . . . Lord bless us. It's all your no-good father's fault. Drunkards breed disease, water on the brain and all sorts of falling fits. Epilepsy, say . . . that's an innocent sounding name for a drunkard's disease. That it is."

Grandma went to the kitchen to insult drunkards some more, and Leena was left alone with her epilepsy. Epilepsy, pepilepsy, eppy-peppy-leppy . . . She tasted the word on her tongue and became fond of it.

A FEW DAYS WENT BY, and Leena was still in bed. Grandma looked on her recovery in distress, almost in terror: she was terrified by the disease, which wasn't a normal human disease and had an unknowable essence and origin she couldn't figure out—although the daddy drunkard toying around with music, a failure by all accounts, was a good enough origin for any malicious thing that appeared in Leena. In her heart she knew that if she were to waste her tenderness on the sickly child, she would extinguish her painful attachment to all those deceased who no longer needed her attachment—but she was too tired, she had once spent all her tenderness, along with her tears, which only rarely gave her relief anymore. And these dead ones— the crippled first-born who had died as an infant; then her daughter, Leena's mother, who had brainlessly gotten mixed up with the no-good musician and died of childbirth before even entering into matrimony; Matias who had sunk into the sea, the restless dreamer of a man with no inclination for studying; and lastly the husband, a strangely

31

emotional carpenter who had driven away the proud son in a fit of anger, and then, after the son had drowned, had hanged himself from the oven's flue chain—all of them kept her in their magic circle, and she mourned them like we never mourn the living.

So she had nothing but her agitation to give Leena, the agitation that was doubled by the vague insight that she couldn't understand this extraordinary child. As for the fact that her own bottomless suffering radiated to the child and had muddled the calm of her soul from the beginning, that was an even vaguer notion, a mere hunch.

But to Leena herself the days of her recovery were fruit-ful: she had a wonderful time with her miraculous disease. As a matter of fact the only miracle shown her by the dis-ease was not having to go to school for a while. She was utterly happy about that and considered it a credit to the miracle doctor who had guessed that she had pepilepsy, which was the fancy name for her disease. Pepilepsy had brought along other good things, too: she was able to rest, all by herself, look out the window, and *think*—and then she had received a letter from Uncle Eevertti. The letter had also made Grandma so happy that she stopped singing hymns for a whole day, at least not those gloomy hymns that Leena dreaded; on that day she only sang hymns of praise. And she was baking wonderful food: meatballs and pretzels and pie—even though Eevertti Anselmi had written that he would be home in twenty days, Grandma began to wait right away.

But so did Leena. And overwhelmed by happiness, she listened to the pots singing and the sound of Grandma's steps in the kitchen. She had always liked those homely sounds, it was like they were proof of Grandma's existence: that she was *real*, fully alive—not the being that sorrow had faded into a hymn-singing shadow, wandering along the river of death.

How strange it was that it was hard to believe in the existence of the people closest to you, unless there was proof. Today she had received proof from Eevertti Anselmi, a fetching love letter. She kept rereading it, little by little, slowly spooning joy out of the letter like dessert. Uncle could write such lovely letters that his missus had once— when she had read one of Leena's letters on a visit—become jealous and had never gotten over her spite. That actually pleased Leena; she didn't care to be on friendly terms with a woman who addressed Eevertti with such hurtful sugaring as "my husband" or "my dear Eevertti"—for surely Eevertti Anselmi was rather Leena's man than hers, since she had known her Eevertti eight years longer than that dubious woman, who had ended up with Uncle quite by chance before publicly become his missus.

And in order to relieve her envious heart, she pulled out the letter from under her pillow and read again:

Hear me, my little Leena,

Is it true that you have fallen ill again? It does not suit our plans at all, and we won't have it. I will come to town on my holiday soonishly, and then we will make you all better again. Believe me?

For the time being, you must take good care of yourself, obey the law to the letter. And I would naturally be very happy if you wrote me—about everything that's going on in your head and heart. For a great many things are obviously going on there since you are such a clever poet.

Clever indeed. Once, as a little girl, when you saw a toad for the first time in your life, you showed it to me in awe and said, "Look, look, a poo is jumping!" That was poetry, and good poetry at that. Better than usual.

And once you found a wonderful flower in Grandma's violet bed, like none you had seen before. It was like velvet, and you could not help touching it—but then the flower flew off. Remember?

You ran to me and told me what you had seen. And I laughed and told you that you had seen a butterfly. And you asked me, why did Grandma not plant butterflies in every flowerbed since they were so beautiful, and could fly, too. And I laughed again, and said that butterflies weren't flowers but insects, like flies or gnats.

You didn't answer to that, but I could see that you were very sorry and upset on behalf of the butterfly. I understood that you thought insect too drab a word, and that "fly" and "gnat" ruined everything. I also understood that the butterfly was a very special creature to you, almost like an angel, and it had a special message for you.

See, this letter is a kind of modest butterfly, a little paper angel with a message for you. Firstly: I will be on leave in exactly twenty days, and then we'll have a long talk about everything. Secondly: you may wish for anything you want—as long as it's not a polar bear or zeppelin—and your wish will be considered promptly.

Your Uncle Eevertti.

Leena let out a sigh of happiness and fell into dreams of Eevertti Anselmi. First she pictured his teeth. Eevertti had two very big and funny front teeth—just like a rabbit. She loved her uncle especially for those teeth. For Uncle's most tender gesture was to bite her ear.

Then a gloomy suspicion sneaked into her heart. Eevertti Anselmi also sometimes bit the ear of Mona Lisa, his impossibly sweet and gigantic dog—and Leena didn't mind that, of course. But what if—what if someone other than her or Mona also received Uncle's special tenderness? What if he bit his missus's ear, too?

It was horrible—horrible. Leena couldn't bear the idea. But surely it wasn't possible. Bite the missus . . . No, if Eevertti Anselmi did perhaps love his missus, he could not love her by biting her ear. The missus was a necessity in Uncle's life, just like school was a necessity in Leena's. The missus was a necessary but somehow official woman and thus Eevertti Anselmi's love for his missus was also necessary and official, not private and exciting in the same way as the love he and Leena shared.

This is how it had to be, and Leena made do with it. Still, there was a melancholy suspicion nagging at her, and the day that had begun beautifully was now ruined. Even Eevertti's letter didn't feel as charming as before; it was a very courteous letter, but the glimmer was gone. What had Eevertti said, again? That she might make a wish, wish for anything. What could she wish, then? Nothing—she had no wishes.

She felt a dull disappointment as she realized she couldn't wish for anything. Well, there was one thing, but she couldn't ask Eevertti Anselmi for that: to *always* have the falling sickness and never have to go to school.

YET SHE DID HAVE TO GO back to school. Before she knew it, she was back in the ugly classroom, sitting at her ink-stained desk, afraid. She was not afraid of the teacher in particular—the teacher was simply the embodiment and continuous object of her all-embracing fear, as well as a metaphor for it—nor was she especially afraid of her peers, either, though she shunned their company and flinched at them. If someone had asked her what she was afraid of, she would have found it impossible to answer; she was just overwhelmed by some disintegrating terror that she couldn't explain and that made her blind and deaf to everything else.

"Leena!"

Leena jumped up, startled. She had no idea what the teacher had asked.

"Why didn't your grandmother come by when I asked her to? Did you give her my letter?"

Leena had not learned to lie yet.

"The letter . . ." she mumbled. "No, I made a bird out of it, and . . ."

"You did what?"

The tone of the teacher's voice did not bode well. Leena wanted to tell her truthfully that the letter had wanted to turn into a bird and fly, but somehow she intuited that the answer would not be acceptable to the teacher. That's why she quickly said, not knowing how she got the words out: "I threw it out."

But she knew that wasn't the *real* truth, and her heart ached.

Silence. Then the teacher opened her mouth and said: "You did what?"

"I don't . . . know," said Leena in a muddy voice.

"So you did not give the letter to your grandmother?"

"No . . ."

"Is that so! Well, let's move on to the next matter. You have been absent for a week. Bring me your excuse!"

Leena didn't have it. Grandma had told her to explain that she didn't really know what had been wrong with her, and that her uncle would come to school to discuss it in a couple of weeks, and then everything would be nicely straightened out. Grandma herself didn't have much talent for speaking; besides, it seemed like she thought there was something awful about the falling sickness, something unfathomable, hence shameful, so it had to be kept a secret. If Leena did have the falling sickness after all.

"Well, Leena? Don't you have an excuse?"

"No, because Grandma . . . Grandma was too tired to write. But Uncle . . ."

"What about Uncle?"

"Uncle will come in two weeks and . . ."

"That's not good enough. I want your excuse now, not in two weeks. Is your grandma sick?"

"No . . ."

"Well, then there should have been no reason for not writing a note. It's easy enough to write a line or two."

Leena had nothing to say to that.

"Listen," said the teacher in an almost pious tone. "What's the meaning of all this? You've been playing hooky, is that it?"

The class was shaking in anxious anticipation.

"I have not," stated Leena, tears filling her throat.

"Well, what does this behavior mean then? If you had been sick, your grandma would have sent an honest explanation. First you destroy my letter and then you come to school with no excuse. How can you explain that? Speak up, please!"

"I was sick," said Leena and started crying.

"Sick how?" prompted the teacher.

Leena cried and cried without a word.

"Crying isn't going to help now, and there's no use lying. I will ask you one more time: why have you been absent from school? What was wrong with you?"

"I don't know." Leena worried the handkerchief in her fingers and let out a long sob.

The teacher sighed in despair.

"You wear me out. Sit now, I'll think about what should be done with you. Oh, no—you can't go to sleep again, you never listen to the lesson. It's better to give you an errand— let's see if you can manage even that. I left my eyeglasses in the natural history room. You go get them—they're in the teacher's desk. But hurry!"

"Where's the natural history room?" asked Leena, utterly unhappy.

The class laughed in unison.

"What? You have gone to school for almost two months and don't know that, even though it's on this same floor? Please go find it, now!"

Leena went. She felt the eyes of all her classmates on her back and zigzagged between the desks like a rabbit. She closed the door soundlessly behind her and stood there helplessly. The corridor was distressingly deserted, frozen still and dead. Its ugliness had gained a kind of eternity, a terrible finiteness. Now that the stir and bustle of recess was gone, the corridor was somehow supernaturally dismal and absolutely ugly.

Filled with horror, Leena tiptoed from door to door, reading the signs above them: 3rd class, 4th class, Staff Room, School Board. She heard loud laughter through a door—the liberated as well as cruel, totally uninhibited laughter of the whole classroom community. Leena ran away, startled, and finally she came to the door, above which there were the deadly serious words: Natural History Lecture Room. She stopped behind the door to listen. Silence.

Unwillingly, she pressed the door handle and stepped over the threshold. And she had a vague notion that she had crossed some important line, and that her world was about to change on the other side.

There wasn't a soul in the room, yet it wasn't empty, Leena felt that instinctively. The students were gone; the pack was gone but the spirit was left—left behind was the constant labor and the frantic struggle of the classroom's social structure, the cruel laughter and odd excitement and restlessness mixed with fear that nested in every classroom, that stuck in them. The group was gone but the torture was still there.

Leena wandered to the back of the class mechanically, and stopped by the teacher's desk. It was the same shape as a writing desk, and the years had drawn cryptic characters on it. The ink stains, scratches, initials—all of that was mystic scripture, secret writing she couldn't read but found tantalizing like everything with a hidden meaning. Standing there, by the stained desk, she felt a little like she had felt when she first held the alphabet book in her hand. And then she had an irresistible urge to add her own mark in the ABCs drawn by time.

In the recessed pencil holder on the desktop she discovered a pair of compasses and found them a fitting tool. She would rather have scraped her whole name into the wood—Saara Magdaleena Muisto Susanna, class II B— but she knew it would cause a racket and she would have to stand in the corner again to pay for her crime. So she only scraped a modest L on the desk, but did her deed deeply conscious of her calling, with hot hands and a throbbing heart. Great, she said to herself, when her work was done and she looked at her symbol, limp and a little broken, but utterly artistic, all the same. God will know that it means me. God knows—and so do I. God and I, and that's all that matters.

The eyeglasses! She had forgotten all about them. She now felt an urgency to look for them. She had no more time to admire her work so she opened the desk and peeked inside. There was all sorts of stuff; toys confiscated from the students were among the best things, but there were also truly mysterious objects whose purpose Leena didn't know. The teacher's eyeglasses were also there, with the metal earpieces, knowing and important looking and hateful because she had to touch them. What if—what if she dropped the glasses, broke them before she could get them to the teacher? Dropped them like she had dropped the ink bottle because she was scared of dropping it and her fears always came true? The teacher would surely kill her then.

With sweaty, shaky hands she lifted the glasses. At the same time her lips tried to say a prayer, to chant the words whose help she had no longer believed in after the accident with the ink bottle had happened. Dear God, don't let it happen, hold on to the glasses, if you have the time, I mean . . . But suddenly the fear was forgotten, and the prayer, and along with it the eyeglasses; she had discovered something that drew her like a magnet. Among the junk in the desk glimmered a small metal hoop, on the inside were round balls side by side, shiny and smooth like pearls.

She stared at the ring, enchanted. She didn't know what it was and what it did, but it worked on her like a talisman. Her fingers grabbed the ring and began to caress it. Every ball was like a pearl, perfect and faultless. She saw her reflection on every ball, small enough to almost disappear, yet perfect and faultless. Seven tiny little likenesses of

Leena—the ring showed her picture seven times at once.

Leena smiled fondly, and the smile caught on every ball. And then she remembered what she had been told of God and the stars and the universe: that the Earth was a star and the universe the starry garden, that every star resembled a ball and that God held them all in his hand. And now she was holding the seven balls, the seven stars in her own hand, her smile caught on the stars, and she could look at her picture on every one of them.

Charmed, she put her toy on the desk and looked at the ring that connected the balls, connected the smile and the stars. She pushed it with her finger—and it rolled on. It moved! The ring moved by itself! And it obeyed her steering finger, supply and easily, playfully. She could move it all she wanted, steer it wherever she wanted. The ring obeyed her, the magic ring and these seven balls, seven small worlds.

Then she knew she would take the ring, take it without asking for permission. She wanted it for herself, wanted it in some omnipotent way that knew no hindrances and made all laws and teachings lose their meanings.

She had decided to steal the ring, and her conscience did not make a sound. No, she was so wholly and fully overjoyed that her conscience sang with her.

And she slipped the ring under her sleeve and left the room very happy and brave, the universe with her.

WHEN SHE GOT BACK to her own classroom the old fear overwhelmed her again. The perpetual blame and reproach in the teacher's eyes made her feel rotten—yet she didn't even remember she had committed a crime. She quickly set the eyeglasses on the teacher's table, curtsied awkwardly, and started rushing, almost running, to her desk.

"Leena! Where have you been this long?"

Leena had just sat down but the teacher's voice made her hastily get up.

When she was startled she always lost her composure, this time too. Something slid from her sleeve and fell on the floor, rattling. In her ears it sounded like an explosion.

The silence that followed the explosion was not broken even by the breathlessly, anxiously anticipating class. Leena was frozen, staring at the metal ring lying in the middle of the aisle. Then she saw the teacher climb down from the lectern and move towards her. It took her an eternity to reach the ring. Finally she stopped, picked up the stolen thing off the ground and said in an unnaturally calm voice:

"Where did you get this?"

For the first time some new force took over Leena's fear: the will to defend herself. Her hands were sweating and her brain was bursting: she was trying to think.

"Answer me, Leena!"

Leena kept swallowing; she wasn't used to thinking while answering for mischief.

"Did you hear me? Answer!"

"I . . . nowhere," said Leena feebly because she hadn't thought it through yet.

The teacher raised her voice.

"I'm asking you for the last time: where did you get this?"

"I . . . I made it."

She was lying for the first time in her life, and that's why she did it so stunningly badly.

"You? Do you know what this thing is?"

The teacher was more puzzled than angry.

"It's a . . . car."

"Car?"

"Yes, a car that moves by itself."

"Hmm. And you've made this—car—yourself. Poor child, you're either remarkably wicked—or not in your right mind."

Now the cheer of the class broke out, finally.

Leena's heart was racing, but she decided to lie bravely till the end. And this time the laughter gave her strength.

"It's not ready yet but it *will* be a car," she said almost passionately.

"Is that so! And because of this you'll receive a lowered mark for behavior," said the teacher with the air of calm that only hopelessness can bring. "This car made by your own hands is a ball bearing and it was in the physics teacher's desk. There will be consequences—you little thief. Now sit down!"

Leena sat. A thief . . . Yes, it was true; she had stolen the ring, but she wasn't sorry. She was only sorry for getting caught and losing her treasure.

But she had no time to worry about that now. She had something else to occupy her: hating the teacher. If she had hated the teacher up till now, the hatred had arisen from fear and been vague and confused. Now she hated with determination and persistence, because she *wanted* to hate. The teacher had killed a part of her, and she could feel it.

So she sat there hating, hating bitterly and not feeling a pang of conscience, until the bell finally gave her mercy. Through the rustle of the rows of pupils getting up, she could hear the teacher's unwavering voice:

"Today's Saturday, and Monday is the monthly holiday.

I have to come here in the evening anyway, to correct exercise books, and you'll accompany me. You must be here in this room Monday at eight p.m. You get two hours of detention and a lowered mark for behavior. You may go now."

As soon as Leena got away from the teacher and the school, the hate turned into sorrow and tears. When she got home, she sneaked right into the bedroom and climbed into the rocking chair to pity herself. She always shared her self-pity and sorrow generously and faithfully with her little cat named Samuel. It wasn't a real cat, it was just a black rabbit-fur collar, worn and scabby, but when the mood was right it performed the role perfectly. And Leena squeezed Samuel to her and wept into his fur:

"You're the best person in the whole world!"

Samuel didn't answer, poor Samuel didn't even purr like an engine, the way ordinary mortal cats do, but maybe just for its silence it could so compassionately feed Leena's sorrows. This unusual cat's biblical name was after a little Jewish boy who had once lived by the yard; the boy had been wild and beautiful and dirty, and Leena had probably loved him the most for his dirtiness. Leena felt it was somehow bold and brave, as she herself had to adjust to washing every morning and carefully minding her skirt on the littered back alleys.

It had been exciting, anyhow, for Samuel could turn any old game into adventure and make up shockingly sweet stories. And he could swear in Hebrew. Kiss my soul and Jupiter's arse, he said in a horrible voice, and it was Hebrew and it meant awful things. The grown-ups kept warning Leena, saying that the boy was a liar and a weasel, but the grown-ups got it backwards, because Samuel's weaseling was romantic, so it was appropriate.

But then Samuel had moved away from their yard. It had happened in the same sad autumn when their regular organ grinder stopped coming. Until then the man had come to their yard almost every week and ground the world's most beautiful tunes out of the box that could sing. The box was old just like the player, but if you had a bit of imagination, it didn't matter that the dreaming of the hurdy-gurdy now and then died down to a melancholy whistle. "Oh, my dearest Augustin, all is gone, gone . . ." And the barrel organ sighed so that the heart was about to burst.

Leena gave a sob and pressed her face into the rabbit pelt that smelled just like Samuel, the original one. And the rocking chair moved slowly back and forth and its rockers meowed out the rhythm of a dreamed music and old memory.

The years have gone by,
The bird cherry perfume—
Youth has long ago passed us by . . .

The busker had always conjured this song out of his box as his last number, to fulfill Leena's wish, even when she didn't have a ten-penny coin to give.

And Leena mourned the ten-penny coins that she could not give, mourned the barrel organ, the music, and Samuel, who had all abandoned her. Or had they? She heard the old sentimental tune as clearly as if it had been playing under the window, and the music lulled her to its own timeless atmosphere where the uninterrupted movement of the rocking chair was heard from somewhere very far away: back-and-forth, back-and-forth, back-and-forth.

She rocks on and on, the music fading and thinning out, and suddenly she's loose from everything and floating freely in the air, space, the never-ending emptiness. Then an odd thought awes her: what if this rocking never ends, what if she drifts like this forever . . . Like the chubby-cheeked angel of a Victorian scrap that can never get down from the cloud. The thought is horrifying to her, and she wants to pray to God to take eternity away from her, so that she wouldn't have to become an angel and rock on the cloud endlessly, but she knows the prayer is no use, because surely God's on eternity's side, against her.

And so she climbed off the rocking chair, crawled onto the sofa, and buried her head in the cushions. She never wanted to be an angel. She never wanted to go to Heaven. She never again wanted to rock in a rocking chair and think about eternity. She wanted to think of nothing. She wanted to cease existing, die forever.

She wanted to die but death didn't come when you prayed for it. It didn't just come. And she didn't want a random death. She wanted a death she could decide on.

And maybe now was a good time to decide. She had lived far too long, terribly long, longer than she wanted to remember. When she thought of her life she didn't truly remember any of it. She only saw a row of days, ash gray days, some rare spots of color between them, and they meant nothing to her. The only thing that meant something was death. She dreamed of it; and her shapeless grief was relieved; she held it in her hands like some strange bird.

For this blissful death of hers was in her own hands. It was not an ordinary death, because it obeyed her wishes. It didn't matter if the whole world was against her; with her death she'd do whatever she wanted—today, tomorrow, whenever she pleased.

Would do . . . How would she do it? She hadn't thought

of that because she could postpone her death as long as she wanted.

But now it couldn't be postponed any longer. After what had happened at school, death was a necessity, and faced with this necessity, Leena felt a fierce, hot terror.

But a new knowledge grew from the root of her terror like a strange and wonderful blossom: God would let her know what she needed to do. She'd go to church tomorrow, sit there all day if she had to, and wait for God's word.

And she promised to God that she wouldn't get bored in church, if God showed her an angel or some other heavenly apparition. She was now trying God, demanding a sign or word, and she felt that God had to answer her.

Leena didn't mention her plan to Grandma. When Sunday came she took a big red ball and pretended to go play outside. The yard was absolutely silent and deserted; it was church time, and that's when people napped. There was nobody in sight; the houses, the old yellow wood buildings looked strangely closed off and dead, like they'd gone to eternal sleep. Cart-track plants and low wild chamomiles grew between the cobblestones giving the yard a feel of abandon and forgetfulness. And above all this forgetfulness shone the fading autumn sun, shone like an enormous flower or button cut out of aluminum foil.

Leena sneaked across the yard, staying close to the wall so that Grandma couldn't spot her from the window. At the gate she dropped the ball and let it roll onto the street. It bounced into the gutter and started down the gently sloping hill, fast, and Leena went after it. At the corner she caught up with the ball and squeezed it under her arm. "Let's go see angels," she said to the ball. "Let's go see the angels and God."

There was the same stillness on the street as in the yard. Not that the street was deserted and empty; there were a lot of people passing, but they felt oddly unreal, almost like they were sleepwalking. It was like they were walking unthinkingly, unwillingly—like dolls or machines walking automatically. Or maybe that's just how Leena felt. Maybe she was walking unthinkingly, unwillingly herself. Yes, a strange will, from outside her, led her past these people moving like machines, past these houses framing the streets like a facade. And the whole time she was saying, to the ball and herself, "Let's go see the angels. Let's go see the angels and God."

Suddenly she realized that the lighting seemed to be changing and the air was getting cooler and thinner; she had come to the old part of town where the streets were narrower, houses lower, shadows longer. These streets were the *purple streets* to her—perhaps because the color purple represented to her a vague yearning and sadness. She dimly intuited that in the vanishing world of these streets there was at the same time an unthinkable happiness and hope-lessness, love that really belonged to the past. And still the past was present all around here, the past that had built these streets. The people were gone but their yearning was still here.

Strangely enchanted, Leena spelled out the street names—Mustainveljestenkatu, Harmaidenveljestenkatu,

Luostarinkatu, Karjaportti—and she remembered the smile of Saint Francis on the picture postcard on the wall at home. This world was unreal, like a dream or adventure on the pages of a picture book, and yet realer than the whole entire world. By entering this world one entered a dream, and dreams were realer to Leena than the daytime and ordinary life itself. One could imagine an escape from ordinary life, but not from a dream; in dreams everything happened fatefully, unconditionally, there was no alternative. A dream was absolute like some scary, beautiful fairy tale, prewritten, hence so frightening.

But Leena wasn't afraid now. She had reached the most beautiful of all the fairy-tale streets, and she was not afraid. This street began on the hill beneath an old bell tower, and there was a clock in the tower, and the clock had a black face and big coppery numbers that were comically slanted—since everything belonging to dream and fairy tale had to slant a bit, otherwise a fairy tale was not a real fairy tale.

But the numbers of the fairy-tale clock slanted cutely, and if you looked carefully, it seemed that the whole clock tower slanted a bit. And beneath the tower began the narrowest street in the world with passageways that tilted nicely, and the street made a steep decline, and between the cobbles grew wild thyme and sorrel. And at the bottom of the hill there was the sea, and above the sea there was the sky, and between the sea and the sky there was nothing but a thin line that seemed painted in watercolor. And when you looked at that line for a little while from the hilltop, it started shimmering and dispersing, it vanished, and the sea vanished, and the street fell straight to Heaven.

This street was the end of the world, this street was Heaven's pier, and Leena was sure that on dark autumn nights you could pick stars on the beach.

Yes, everything that was possible in a fairy tale was possible on this street. If she were to bump into an angel or Jesus there it wouldn't have surprised her at all. If an angel came along she wouldn't want to go home anymore. She would go after the angel, follow the angel away—where the street fell to Heaven.

By this heavenly street, on the crest of the hill, there was a small white stucco building that could hardly be seen among the thick foliage of the maples. It was a Roman Catholic Church, whose door was always open so that a passerby could stop by anytime. The church was old, modest, and kind just like the whole street where Francis's smile, fairy tale, and legend lived.

The sand on the maple path gleamed almost white under Leena's feet as she quietly tiptoed to the church door. It was a big, heavy oak door, and she couldn't open it on the first try. She squeezed the ball tighter under her arm and grabbed the door handle with both hands. "Let's go see the angels. Let's go see the angels and God." And that's when it happened.

First she thought she had entered Heaven. She didn't see anything right away, just heard an unearthly music. Then her eyes adjusted to the dimness and she made out a dark row of benches and the water-clear light, filtering through small round windows. On the altar at the front of the church there was a big-eyed Madonna with the baby Jesus in her arms and a pigeon on top of her head; the bottomless gaze of the saintly picture drifted through the shimmering light and reached her. However, she saw all this dimly, as a dreamscape for the music that came from above her head, and in that music there was God.

It was hard to believe such music was real. She had never heard anything like it before. It wasn't happy or sad; it was unexplained, yet crystal clear. Unexplained and crystal clear like water—water which is clear like the sky and has no bottom.

That was it. Water was the right word. It didn't say anything, yet it said everything. That's what this music was like. Water and sky—bottomless.

It would be good to die in water like that. Or music like that . . . This was the music Leena wanted to die in.

For she knew she could listen to this music forever, she'd never tire of it—never. And she also knew that if she died in this music she could listen to it for all eternity.

Eternity . . . But then the waters parted and a mountain rose from below like an apparition. The bass boomed. Leena flinched and the ball fell from her hands. Like a strange red animal it went bouncing towards the altar.

Leena froze in the doorway and stared at the ball in awe. The organs thundered above her head but she didn't hear them. She only knew that something was about to happen—that something terrible was about to happen.

Then she saw some black creature move along the aisle lightly like a spirit, carrying the ball. The spirit got nearer and took the form of a penguin. Leena couldn't move but in her mind she prayed to the penguin for mercy.

Then the penguin stopped, and Leena heard a mild voice say:

"Here, take your ball. Come outside and we'll have a little talk."

And she took Leena's arm and led her out of the church in a motherly way.

Leena knew now she didn't have to be afraid anymore.

"I think it's best to leave your ball at home the next time you come to church."

The penguin's voice tried to assume a reproachful tone but her lips were smiling. And her eyes were smiling, too. There was more smile in them than could possibly fit in all the eyes of the world, thought Leena poetically.

Probably her poetic mood didn't show, though, because the penguin asked what had frightened her so badly. Leena tried to say that she wasn't frightened at all anymore but all the words had slipped away, slid from her throat to her stomach, and she couldn't say anything even if she felt a pinch in her stomach. Instead, she stared involuntarily at the extraordinary black cape that made the creature look like a penguin.

"I suppose you're wondering about my habit, aren't you? See, all of us Roman Catholic sisters wear one just like this, in a way it's our uniform. I'm Sister Elisabet—or just Elisabet if you like. And what about you? What's your name?"

"Leena. Or Magdaleena, really. Or Saara Magdaleena Muisto Susanna precisely."

This made Elisabet smile.

"A dear child is given many names. Who has been so generous? Mom?"

Leena looked at the tips of her toes. The sole of her left shoe was torn, and the shoe presented her with a comically lopsided smile.

"I don't have a Mom," she said to her shoe.

"No? Did your mom die? When?"

Leena's mood turned blue. Usually she could talk about her dead mother like any ordinary thing. She couldn't very well mourn a person she had never seen. But now she felt it was the appropriate moment for grief.

"I don't remember," she muttered and made her best sad face.

"Then you must have been very little when your mom died. Right?"

"Three days old, Grandma says." Leena said this in a confident, matter-of-fact way. It sounded like she was repeating a well-learned lesson. But she was still staring at her shoe, and the shoe was grinning. Through its laughter she could hear Elisabet's voice.

"You came to this church on your own?"

"Yes."

"Have you been here before?"

"No . . . This is the first time."

"How did you find your way here, all by yourself? Or do you live somewhere near?"

"I don't know . . . But no, we don't live here, we live behind the market and park and school and the madhouse." Leena was still talking to her broken shoe, and the shoe patiently smiled and helped her go on:

"I was going to go to the big church, the ordinary one

with the tower and the priest in the pulpit and a basket and all that, but . . ."

"But?"

"Someone took me here . . . No one, I mean," she added helplessly, puzzled.

"Really, that's exciting. And nice, of course. I mean that it's nice that Someone-No-one took you here. And—did you like our church?"

"I did . . . so much," Leena sighed. "The music . . . it was like . . ."

"Like what?"

"Water," Leena said feebly.

"You're right. Music is the living water and that's the water God writes on."

Leena's eyes were shining. She was happy that she was so easily understood.

"What was it, that music?" she asked almost fervently.

"It was Bach. One of Bach's fugues. You can meet the musician, too, if you want."

"Bach?"

"No," laughed Elisabet. "Bach has been dead for almost two hundred years. But you can meet Brother Filemon, the organ player."

Leena was so overjoyed that she forgot all about civilized reserve.

"I know a cat named Filemon," she said excitedly like she had thought of a common acquaintance. "He lives in our yard and is very wise."

"Our Filemon is very wise, too. He . . ."

"And he has a face like a chimney sweep's, and one of his ears was bitten off in a fight."

"Oh, the poor old veteran. Well, our Filemon likes little girls and he can play for you, whatever you want. Leena, can you play music? Do you have an instrument?"

"Inst— . . . I only have this ball."

Sister Elisabet laughed.

"Yes, though one cannot play music with a ball. But maybe you'd like to learn to play? Say, Bach?"

Leena felt dizzy.

"What they just played in church?" she asked breathlessly.

"Yes, among others."

"But . . . I could never learn to play that."

"Of course you can. Look, Bach is like a great big mountain, and most people pass by the mountain without seeing it because it's too big and too close. But you saw it and got it and were ready to fall in love with Bach the very first time you heard him. That's why I'm positive you're a very gifted child. You know that?"

Leena was almost frightened. She squinted, her eyes

looking black and wild out of sheer surprise, and she didn't look gifted at all.

"Trust me, I know. Come, I'll show you something."

And she took the girl's hand and led her to the back of the garden where a small white stucco hut was hidden under a maple. By the wall there was a thin strip of a flowerbed with a few late-blooming violets.

"The janitor lives here, and this is his garden," explained Elisabet. "Look at these violets, they're very beautiful, every one of them is like a poem, risen from the soil . . ."

" . . .that God has made up. In his own head," Leena completed quickly.

"In his own head, yes. But there's something sad about them, isn't there? And do you know why they're so sad?"

No, Leena didn't know that. But looking at the flowers made her frown in compassion. On the little velvet faces of violets there really was such a sad and unhappy look it made you quite blue.

"Yes, they're so sad because they don't know how beautiful they are."

Leena understood. The autumn sun was tilting behind the roofs, and the thinning light made the velvet-faced, poem-like flowers look all the more sad and beautiful. Sister Elisabet went on:

"Well, the same goes for you. You don't know how

gifted you are, and that's why you're so sad. Understand, Leena? Do you believe me when I tell you I'm sure you have the most extraordinary talent for music?"

"I don't know," mumbled Leena shyly, but she was absolutely delighted and felt a boundless gratitude for Sister Elisabet, who had given her the most extraordinary talent for music, just like that. And she thought that now that she had found Sister Elisabet, she couldn't really be that unhappy ever again. For she felt that along with the amazing musical talent she had been given something much more important and unbelievable: a mother, a real, live mother. Or almost real, at least, she added to herself, overcome by a blurry fear of loss. The bad thing named The Ordinary that was lurking behind every corner, feasting on rosy dreams, eating their wings and leaving just the carcasses, warned her not to get carried away, so she had to give away a little of her happiness. Although the fact that she now had an almost real mother really was lovely enough to scare her. Almost-Mom. Pretend Mom. Angel Mom, Angel Mom! She had gotten an Angel Mom just like that, out of the blue. Fallen from Heaven, and for free. Like a Victorian scrap she had once been given at Naukkarinen stationary shop—just as surprising and free.

"Like a scrap paper," she sighed aloud, dizzy with happiness.

But right then she came to think that surely this cannot be true. Surely she must be dreaming—like usual, like always—and the Angel Mom, too, was just dream and imaginary from the very beginning. So she squeezed her eyes shut with all her might—but when she looked around again, here was Elisabet the same as before, the church the same, and she the same herself; everything was the same or looked the same, at least. Only the lighting had changed; it had a weirdly greenish and glass-like hue, as if someone had put the sun in a hidden green bottle.

And then she felt the earth shake underneath her like she was standing on a wooden bridge, the sky was shaking like it was made of paper, and the walls of the houses were wavering like the cardboard houses of a theater set; everything shook rhythmically, in silence, and she thought that maybe it was all just a dream after all and maybe the dream went on—went on stubbornly, despite everything. Perhaps it would go on forever.

But she felt dizzy and scared, and frantically she asked Elisabet:

"Tell me, are you really real?"

"Real? What do you mean—real in what way?"

"An angel," Leena whispered. She would rather have said "Angel Mom" but she was afraid of offending Elisabet and thus her secret dream.

Elisabet laughed joyfully.

"Angel? Me? Surely not! Really . . ."

Leena felt even more panicked.

"What shall I do then?" she asked, overwhelmingly unhappy. But at the same time she realized her question hadn't really been answered yet, so she tried again:

"I mean is this real, *really real*?"

This made Elisabet look so strange that Leena felt she had to help out a little more.

"Or maybe everything's just a dream?" she almost whispered.

"Everything?"

"Yes," Leena said, her eyes black with nervousness and fear.

"You mean that maybe life's just a dream, right?"

"I mean that . . . Is it true that you're standing there and I'm here and we're alive? Is *this* true, tell me?" Leena's voice was passionate.

"I don't seem to quite understand you just now," said Elisabet a little uncertainly, bewildered by the girl's stare. Then she added, laughing, "But don't worry, we'll ask Brother Filemon if all this is real or not."

"But what if he doesn't know, either? What'll we do then?" Leena almost cried out.

Elisabet looked at her, startled, and for a moment it

seemed that the girl's unnatural terror was catching. Then she realized how senseless and comical it all was, but to please Leena she said in a serious voice:

"You can ask Filemon yourself. Here he comes."

FILEMON WAS A SMALL, bearded, shriveled old man, so shriveled that even the beard looked more alive than the rest of him. The beard was bushy and bold and almost snow white—not counting the few suspicious-looking stains whose origins Leena couldn't guess. He had a mustard-yellow linen coat and pants that had faded to an indistinct color and flopped comically as he swayed down the church stairs, leaning on a cane with a hooked end. Somehow this cane was an integral part of the man, the cane and the old man seemed to be the same, carved out of the same piece of wood. The cane was bigger than life, and seemed to know it; it had a very knowing, important look about it. And for good reason: Leena could see right away that it walked the man, not the other way around.

Another addition to the picture was a dog-like animal that looked like a woolly pig or a sack of flour: as it wobbled after its master, it appeared to be rolling, since it was hard to see its feet underneath its belly. It was probably a dog that had eaten too much and come to resemble a living flour sack. Leena, however, believed it was probably a flour sack that had too much imagination and came to think it was a dog.

"Hello Elisabet, my herb garden, virginal and fenced off!" shouted the old man in a loud voice that could have made mountains waver. It was hard to believe that a small person who seemed to hardly draw breath could make such a great, mighty sound, so Leena instinctively looked at the dog who was toddling along at the old man's heel. But the dog wasn't speaking, his mouth was shut and stayed shut, and Leena felt rather disappointed when the old man went on in his booming voice:

"Do you know everything about the mystery of wine and blood—and, if possible, more? You don't? Well, I do. When I in my boundless self-loathing and Christian love for Bacchus—"

"Quiet," said Elisabet urgently, and her tone carried fright and offense.

"Ah, I see that my divine sister is prudently piqued and modest. How lamentable that it's the duty of so many to be prudently piqued and modest. Or, not lamentable at all, if it helps along the coming about of their heavenly bliss.

Thus I, too, vomited by our Lord, a wretched soul called to perdition, I help along the bliss of the world, and sin for God's great honor. Yes, and for the happiness of those who with their practice of virtue are deserving their future home in Heaven."

"Filemon—"

"I hear you. But why this disapproving tone and lack of confidence? See, I've always respected honest salesmen and deserving hard work—"

"Stop!" commanded Elisabet, and Leena realized that angels, too, could get indignant. The old man had been speaking about unholy things in such a pious tone that it came out like blasphemy, but Leena couldn't quite understand the moral dubiousness of the matter; she was just amused by the old man's stories. At home she had heard such bad and bitter words about sin that she was tired of the rottenness and importance of it, and she found it amusing to meet someone who was apparently at ease with such an inevitable, everyday thing as sin. Most of all she found it fun to watch the old man's beard shake as he spoke.

"Look here," said Elisabet to the old man, by way of explanation, "we have a guest, Leena."

"A goddamn girl?" said the old man, glancing at Leena suspiciously. Then he limped to the weathered garden bench and fell down so heavily that the bench squeaked in complaint, and the dog-like creature who had listened to his speech standing with adoring eyes also sat down, curling up at his feet.

"A girl, is it?" The old man's long, white fingers that looked absurdly lively and young compared to his aged and worn appearance found a large dotty handkerchief in his jacket pocket and conjured a tobacco pouch and a pipe from its folds. The fingers fondled the pipe, conscious of the importance of the work, even gently, and an almost tender look passed over the old man's face. Then he stuck the pipe into the hole in the beard, took off his expression and said in an irritated tone:

"I don't like children, not at all! And I don't like paradoxes. Not paradoxes that make sense, anyway."

"What are you on about?" asked Elisabet, bemused.

"Aha, 'what are you on about' since you're such a child yourself, a backward, stunted child? Sure I am, if you like, and of course you do, as you like everything sterile. I still don't like children. I don't like those who go against reason, who have a different reason to mine, that is. They make me feel like an idiot, damn it."

Leena was puzzled and looked at the old man, who resembled Moses or Santa Claus. Santa went on:

"Children are inhuman beings, help me God and protect me from them. Walking around with their heads full of questions, terrible questions, and what's worse is you have to try and answer them. Hell, I could just as easily answer the questions of a mouse or lobster."

"Stop with the wisecracks," asked Elisabet, "and don't scare Leena with your ugly, uh . . . paradoxes."

"I'm not scaring her, but you. Yeah—sure I swear, god-damn it, by ear, and just for the sake of rhythm. You can't ask me to sin against rhythm, you just can't, so I choose the lesser of the two evils. You might want to recall that small vices are much less dangerous than small virtues, goddamn it. Secondly, I'm not babbling wisecracks, I'm just thinking. Swearing is a small vice, thinking even smaller, as long as it doesn't become a habit, God have mercy. And if it had become a habit with me . . . oh well, what then? I'm a weak old man after all. Naturally—naturally I do throw in a wisecrack every now and then, I'll give you that. But try to be generous, at least about small matters, for appearance's sake: I must speak and look wise, or I'll grow donkey ears. For deep inside I'm quite pure."

"I suppose you are," said Elisabet generously and looked at Leena, bemused. Leena herself was trembling with curiosity. The old man sang his funny words looking so dead serious that Leena was wide-eyed, waiting for the donkey ears to break out at any moment.

"That's right," said the old man. "Deep inside I'm a

virgin. If I didn't have a lamentable inclination for the trouble of thinking, I'd wholly be a virgin. But . . . oh well, it comes with old age: as you stop doing and feeling, you start thinking—so they say. See, instead of a heart I have an old mushroom in my chest, full of germs of thoughts, wiggling like maggots. Soon they'll have finished it, those primitive, little things. Ah, how sad and hilarious: you try to tolerate life for almost a hundred years to learn to construct at least a few beginnings of a thought, and then those embryos, those amoebas eat you alive. Eat away all you want, eat the old mushroom oozing bile and vinegar."

"You should drink less," suggested Elisabet. "And talk less. You talk so much and say so little. Say something to Leena here—explain to her if life . . . Yes, if life's real or a dream. That's what she's come here to ask."

The old man's beard looked angry but the pipe that had been stuck into the beard puffed, gurgled, and twittered happily. Overwhelmed by a dim hope and fear, Leena looked at the pipe from whose root she expected to hear the truth and the words of redemption.

"Damn it, I knew it! The mouse starts asking questions. Well, sure I can explain, but whether my explanation will do is another matter. Life's mathematics—counting, that is. I should know, shouldn't I, as I know Bach and Buxtehude by heart. At least my fingers do. When Bach's spirit enters the pipes and touches his chosen souls in a mathematically exacting way, befitting the Lord's intentions . . . But what of it? Petteri knows it, too. Petteri, Pumpkin, Honey Cakes knows . . ."

The dog referred to as Honey Cakes lifted his head and gave his master a grateful look.

"Filemon is trying to wiggle out of it. He doesn't dare say he doesn't know," said Elisabet, noticing Leena's unhappy expression. "He's all about counting, so he thinks life's the same."

"Yeah," said Filemon looking satisfied, and drew bitter smoke out of his pipe.

"Yes, but is it *true*?" asked Leena, short of breath. She had forgotten about her problem for a while, forgotten to worry, but now her concern grew greater again.

The old man seemed amused by the girl's expectant fretting and he laughed to himself, a strangely virile, purring laughter.

"Oh, is it true? Well, that depends on how you look at it. True when it comes to dreams, nonsense when it comes to reality—lies all the same." Then he seemed to get mad at either the stupid questions or his own stupidity and said angrily: "And bloody hell, what about it? Isn't it all the same if life's a dream or reality or some other baloney? You have to get through it anyway, no matter what."

Leena was immensely disappointed and couldn't say anything.

"Well!" prompted the old man and prodded her with his knee. "Isn't it all the same to you whether you're awake or asleep as long as you get to be in your own shoes and be Leena?"

"No," said Leena in her absolute voice. She seemed quite sure.

"No?" said the old man, looking curious. "Why not? Oh well, why am I asking you? Reality is a life of misery—if it indeed qualifies as life at all—and all timely tasks and other erroneous errands, so shockingly important, mockingly shockingly sensible, sure. Reality has a bitter flavor—quite so, I agree. You have good taste, you get an A, dreaming is better."

"No." Leena let the word fall from her mouth like a stone. "Dreaming is worse."

"Worse? I'll be! How might you explain that?"

Leena stared ahead through black eyes, did not utter a word.

"Spit it out!" begged the old man, Filemon. "One has to pull an answer out of you like water from a dry well."

"You can't kill yourself in a dream," said Leena in a strangely loud and prepared voice, like she had pondered the answer for years.

"Well I'll be damned! This girl's in a hurry to kill!" Filemon laughed so that the beard shook and the pipe gurgled. "Well, then it's all right and just as well that you're living in a dream and not even trying to wake up." Then a cunning look came over him, and lowering his voice he said: "But why not, I just might tell you how to let go of dear life in a dream. Yeah, here's how it's done: you steal the Sandman's umbrella, the big and grand one, and go sail the seven seas. Rock the boat—hey, ho—over the railing you'll be sailing, watery bread you'll be tasting, surely baked in water, yeah. Alas, you survive on watery bread, my friend. So I'm afraid you're still hanging on to dear life. But if it's worth the run, it's worth a try, so go follow your calling. And good luck on the way."

Leena was deeply hurt, though not deeply enough. Filemon was so hilariously solemn that she couldn't help laughing, and she felt it would be impossible to get mad at the old man in earnest, even if you wanted to.

Sister Elisabet, though, was quite earnestly shocked by Filemon and Leena's topic of conversation.

"Good Lord," she said, "you're not sending the child off to kill herself, are you? Such talk—from an old man . . ."

Filemon broke out in a great hearty laughter. The laughter gurgled in his throat, sizzled in his beard, wobbled on the hem of his coat and whistled in the pipe bowl. It was a magnificent, impressive laughter, and it caught on everyone and everything, except Elisabet. Then the old man suddenly stopped and looked at Elisabet, outraged.

"Your talk could come out of a sheep's head. If and when and because you're familiar with predestination and other heavenly laws, you should also know that there's no such thing as suicide—other than in thoughts and passions. Fair enough, some kill themselves; it's their way of dying, that's all. You don't even need to be a true believer to get that, all you need is sense. If we can receive a preview of the future—and according to science we can—then the future must somehow already exist somewhere, may the devil know how and where. In other words: there's no future, the future's the past—there you have it, thank you very much. A skilled chemist, scientist, and experimenter whom some call God has prepared everything according to his own ideas and formula, and life is just the result of the experiment, a more or less foul-tasting mixture—sauce, soup, bouillon, salad, or process, call it what you like. Process would be the civilized term."

"You may be right, I don't know. But how does that wisdom help Leena's matters?" asked Elisabet, looking tired of it.

"Of course it doesn't, nothing helps anything, your question is absolutely sorry and sad. I just wanted to say

that there's no such thing as 'Leena's matters.' Anyway,
damn it, they're all like that, each and every one of them.
Heads full of awful questions, extorted from demons and
angels." Filemon's deep voice rose an octave. "Why must
we live? Why is life a Bad Fairy Tale? What happens at the
end? Will the end ever come? Are the angels the same as
the souls of The Innocent? Hell with it, a person with good
sense is not interested in the fate of his soul and innocence.
Ew. But these"—he poked Leena with his cane—"these
inhuman creatures, these human spores with their frail
budding lives want to know about souls and all that, know
everything and more. That's it, even more. They want to
take the soul apart like a mechanical doll and see what's
crying inside. So why's that, damn it? Ho-hum, they hav-
en't gotten used to the dull reality of being, yet—and they
won't get used to it until life stops being a Bad Fairy Tale
and just gets bad. So because they're not used to it, they
want back to where they came from. Where everything's
upside down."

"How can you say 'upside down' with such certainty?"
asked Sister Elisabet. "Or was it a joke?"

"Sure, if you like. Some joke God made up. How can I
say with such certainty? Well, it's just the way of the God-
abiding folks and others bound for salvation. Show me a
good Christian who'd swim without a life preserver. Not

one of them would. I'm sorry and thank you and period and the end. But let's move on, we have evidence, don't we? If I now tell you that on Pilipuu Hill, I met an old hag with her head in a bundle and the bundle under her arm, you'll tell me it's a lie. But Leena here, the mouse, the budding little thing takes me seriously and more than that: to her the hag who carries her head under her arm behaves much more appropriately than the boring human being who keeps her head sensibly but unwisely in the customary place. Who knows where such unnatural and offensive inclination for everything slanted, warped, and mindless comes from—would that be the influence of modern art, say?"

Elisabet seemed to be lost in thought, so joking was no use with her.

"Yes, all I know is that the child *remembers* something we've forgotten—remembers something of the world where the natural order is reversed."

"Who knows? Although you put it coarsely, it nevertheless shows that womenfolk can have sense if they turn their senses around. All right, as you like: like a spruce cone, a child falls into the world where a logical disorder replaces a magical order, and there you are—in trouble, we'll agree. Dimwittedly and inelegantly in trouble. Of course she tries to wiggle and maneuver and make use of her old monkey methods for a while until she learns to use her new, roughly made antennas, learns the civilized ways. That is: until she is tamed, stunted, specializes in humanity, a shame. But— what the hell am I going on about here for?"

The old man yawned, gratified, and the cane scratched the dog-shaped flour bag, which sighed with pleasure. "Soon we'll have trotted the whole way round and then we'll get out, cheers, thanks a lot. You'll get out, too, little Petteri, Pumpkin, Honey Cakes, poor devil. Then there'll be no need to be civilized anymore, no need . . ."

"What happens then? When there's no more need to be . . . like that, civilized?" asked Leena curiously. She had willingly listened to the story of the beheaded hag of Pilipuu Hill and wanted to hear more. "Tell me a story about it, Uncle! A pretty story, Uncle, pretty please."

"Pretty, pretty . . . let's see. If thy Father in Heaven has mercy and lets me choose . . . Shit, all wrong from the beginning. But it's your own fault since you wanted to hear a pretty story."

"Doesn't God have mercy, then?" asked Leena, wide-eyed.

"No. Someone like a king, majesty, or some other official may be merciful as it's a very becoming trait, but our Father accepts no explanations, no foreword, afterword or other excuse. A mere try in that vein is an offense since all tries completely lack style, anyway. Well, in any case he won't let us choose, just so you know."

"Why not?" asked Leena, more out of habit than real passion.

"It wouldn't be economical. Or, to put it more eloquently, it won't do for sheet music. Every key and note and chord and pause has to be put in its exact right place or there'll be no music." The old man smiled wickedly to himself. "Simple and pleasant, huh? So don't get attached to my simplicity, it was a lie from the beginning. But that damn story, the damn pretty story . . . If I could choose, I'd prefer to be a pause. Otherwise my wish list would be very short and humble: a teeny, tiny star out in space— over there where Venus dwells at present, even if you don't happen to see it—a pipe, some Bach, just a little piece but good. Nothing more. I don't care for my head, I'd leave it home. If on that tiny star, see, it happened to be fashionable to carry your head under your arm, it could soon be forgotten, or even exchanged with some absentminded gentleman. Maybe some politician. And that would be a misfortune."

"What's that, a politician? Why a misfortune?" asked Leena unenthusiastically.

"A politician is a Wise Man whose mission is to make the world a better place. Usually he makes it worse than it was to begin with, because a mission's always a misfortune. But that doesn't concern us now, we're concerned with a pretty story—and by the way, the Wise Man's Reason, yes. It is the very best mix of worldly wisdom, and there's a load of it—enough for sheep to eat—and they probably will, so, congratulations. I wouldn't want to be burdened with such great, sane reason even by way of skull exchange; it would be an uncomfortable, risky enterprise. I'd rather take a normal alarm clock than a skull like that."

"A bell-skull like that could be nice. It could play music, too. A waltz, maybe. We used to have one that could . . . but then it broke," Leena reminisced sadly.

"Oh, the waltz machine? Well, it was like the Chinese emperor's man-made nightingale, then. Good, we'll give the machines to the emperors, I'm happy with Bach as cantor."

"But that pipe?"

"Pipe, pipe, concave naturally, of course, thank you for reminding me. A pipe is a light object, it'll fit with something idle, and represent, say, Humor. Or at least irony, in case it pipes down."

All the while chatting, the old man had scooped a bit of clay from under the bench, and while he was answering the girl's questions his fingers were molding the clay in a meditative way. Leena stared at him, charmed. The clay obeyed his fingers, and his thinking fingers gave birth to a bird, it was born easily, just like that, just like from the Heavenly Father's hand. The clay was given wings—wings!

"Here's the answer to all your questions, present and future ones," said the old man in an absentminded tone, finishing the clay bird. "This is what we human beings are capable of creating, some better, some worse, but everyone has a powerful want and need for it. And why not, images turn out, one cleverer than the other—but we can't breathe life into them. About a hundred years ago, when I was a bud just like you now, very fresh and green, with a soul bursting with wings, I watched the Heavenly Father's flying creatures, and one flew right past my nose, twittering and saying 'you do it, you do it'—it said so quite clearly. And I did. My fingers itched for clay before I could even blow my nose properly. I baked birds out of clay, one prettier than the other, and every time I believed with all my might that *this* bird would fly, and when it didn't fly, I burst into tears, ha ha. But"—the old man smiled cunningly and handed Leena the bird—"you teach that sorry bird to fly! Maybe your hands can make the miracle happen."

Leena took the bird, and her heart was singing. The bird's heart was singing, too, singing inside her and inside the clay, and on top of her head, twittering like it was going crazy. And suddenly she realized that the clay bird's heart was beating against her palm—feather-softly and qui-et-quiet, almost like it was afraid, so softly like a feather—and overwhelmed by a burst of joy and tenderness, she squeezed the poor bird so that it suffocated in her hands, along with its song.

"How terrible, I've killed her!" wept Leena, staring unhappily at the clump of clay that had a moment ago been throbbing on her palm. But the old man laughed a good-humored, hearty laugh that made the beard shake.

"Pianissimo, pianissimo, don't break your heart over a piece of clay! That creature didn't breathe, and its throat had no tune in it." Then he went on, his brow knitted, looking almost strict: "Just wait, though . . . A day will come when we learn to make birds that can fly—and chirp like hell." A fantastic whistle escaped out of the old man's pipe. "Like that, chirp-zzrrpp! That's how they compose, like little Mozarts. Zzzrt-t."

"Really?" breathed out Leena, looking at the old man, overwhelmed by a terrible curiosity. "Shall I too . . . learn?"

"Why not, you little monkey—did thy Father in Heaven make you ape him for nothing? To my knowledge it took Pater Noster some practicing before he made the first bird that could fly and make music and lead the way for Mozart—like that, zirrrit!" The old man chatted to his pipe and the pipe knew to answer in Mozart's voice. "And then, then—when the time's right—our turn will come to make birdies out of clay, mold Mozarts, yes. Your turn will come, too; yours. The time of Leena the Believer will come—the time of wings, time of wings—does that inspire you, or what?" The old man's pipe let out a deep sigh. "Then all you need to do is make a wish and open your palm, and Mozart will fly off just like that and begin to compose, out of his mind with joy. A hundred, a thousand, ten thousand winged Mozarts—all out of their minds with joy."

Leena had now completely forgotten about crying, and was staring at the old man bewitched by some passion-filled dream.

"That's right, believe me," the old man continued his testimony, looking stern and weaving his beard. "God went to terrible trouble to make a human being out of a mite—to make Leena out of a mite—sure he won't let all that trouble go to waste, or what do you think?"

Leena had no thoughts on that. Instead she said her dream out loud, breathlessly,

"And can that clay bird fly then, too—the one I squeezed to death? Can't it, Uncle Filemon?"

"Yes, it can," said the old man's hollow bass. "Even stones can fly."

Leena looked at the old man, enchanted. It sounded like the wind had spoken, the wind before an awful earthquake.

Everything was vibrating slowly again, steadily, a rumbling underground current broke out somewhere and the sky tore like paper above her head. A terribly bright light filled the world.

"When?" Leena whispered. She felt dizzy, a glowing light had ignited inside her. The light was like an explosion, it was unbearable, it could kill and surely it would, quite surely it would kill her. "When will it happen?"

"After a million years," answered the old man's bass from very far away, from beyond millions of years. "It's tomorrow. Bach would say tomorrow."

"Tomorrow?" repeated the echo in Leena's shaky voice. Leena was about to die and saw that it had already begun—the earthquake, the end of the world, dying in light.

"Yes. Tomorrow in a million years. It's taken so long to get here, midway, indecently soon. But let's not—let's not fret, let's wait and see . . ."

Then he suddenly banged his cane on the ground, swatted away Bach and millions of years and boomed:

"And let's end it right here. Stop, girl—stop asking questions. Don't make an old man all serious, it's too dull, devilish business, disagreeable and uncomfortable. I won't take on that task."

"Just a moment, Filemon," interjected Elisabet, who had silently looked on as the girl and the old man talked. "Since you're in such a chatty mood, couldn't you shed a little light on those realms of metaphor? In a practical, child-friendly way, of course."

Then the old man Filemon earnestly exploded, got so recklessly and loudly mad that even Leena's earthquake ceased then and there.

"Bloody hell! Metaphor! To hell with all metaphors and seeds of metaphors, I have no use for them! It would be too simple and transparent. I'm not *that* awfully practical, or that child-friendly. I meant exactly what I said—which was a horrible stylistic blunder. I meant . . ."

"Please, Filemon, don't yell . . ."

"I MEANT EXACTLY what I said, and got donkey ears, thank you very much! Be greeted, oh donkey ears, the redeemed innocence! I regret my honesty terribly and awfully and without deceit. I take everything back, right now, entirely. Absolutely everything, except the donkey ears that hold the idyll and idea of perfection. Blessed are the donkey ears: for theirs is the kingdom of metaphor and the everlasting idyll. And blessed be he who is crowned with this miracle and mercy. Come on, Petteri, we've been cheated."

Oozing fiery rage, he gathered his cane and his dog and started limping off to the church, a living creature under both arms.

"Good-bye the lost herb garden, good-bye the lost dream! The transition from man to dream is as long as from mite to man, and there's no neat way to quicken the coming of the dream. There's no style but mere decoration: small virtues and big donkey ears. But let's not throw away your virtue, Elisabet; let it be blessed with the mercy preserved for that purpose. Richly, as it deserves."

Then his eloquent voice turned tender and he went on talking to his dog,

"Petteri, poor devil, Pumpkin, Honey Cakes, let's go, let's go away from misunderstandings and halfhearted morality. Bach is waiting. And Bacchus . . ."

Old man Filemon's fiery exit so bewildered Leena that she completely forgot about the end of the world, forgot she was about to die. The earthquake stopped, just like that, and Leena was back on solid ground.

"Did Uncle really get angry, tell me."

"Not at all, he's quite incapable of getting really angry. He just pretended to be angry."

"Why?" Leena didn't yet understand the art of dissimulation.

"Maybe because deep down he's so very tender-hearted. He has to pretend to get angry so that . . . so that he wouldn't grow donkey ears."

Leena was greatly taken with Filemon's donkey ears and she connected them with everything extraordinary she'd noticed about the old man.

"He was dr— . . . drunk," she said with a wrinkled brow. "Why was he drunk? Because he's so . . . tender-hearted? And so the donkey ears wouldn't grow?"

Elisabet was amused.

"Maybe. Maybe the donkey ears fit here, too. Or . . . maybe he's sad. I don't know exactly."

"Does it help to be drunk if you're sad, then?" Leena's curiosity was the persistent kind.

"You'll have to ask Filemon that one. I don't think it helps, though. But maybe it makes the sadness less gloomy."

"How? Being drunk?" Leena was so confused that it almost made her look like she was guilty of something.

"Well," said Elisabet, sighing, "Filemon says it gives his . . . wretched soul wings."

Wings! A wonderful, blissful word that could alone make its speaker happy and could raise everything into blessed realms. And when it came to being drunk and having wings, she needed to carefully remember this new information. Grandma was always ranting about her father's drinking like it was the cross and curse on the whole world. Now she could help and explain to Grandma that he drank for a good cause. Father wanted wings, wings for his wretched soul.

Just to make sure, she asked Elisabet:

"What does it mean—his wretched soul?"

"It just means his poor soul."

Leena was happy. That's what she had thought. Now she returned to asking about Filemon again.

"Why was he so weird—had a weird look in his eyes, I mean?"

"Did he? Well, I guess so. He's blind, you see. He's been blind many years now."

"Really?" said Leena looking silly and embarrassed. This new surprise was so unexpected that most of all it offended her sense of manners, offended good taste.

"That's right, he can't see anything. Maybe that's why he sees more than many others."

"But how could he make that bird, then? And how . . .?"

"His fingers can see—he's a musician. His fingers have such a fine sense of touch that they never get lost. And he feels his way around, so he can walk like a seeing person."

Leena felt she had a lot to think about, for a long time. Then she remembered the stone and the bird and quickly started asking more questions:

"Did Uncle really mean it when he said that stones will learn to fly, too? Really, really mean it?"

"Yes, he did. Stones will fly—really fly. When that happens the world will be ready."

The world—ready. Leena didn't get Elisabet's promise, but the sentence sounded beautiful.

"Yes. He meant that even a stone aches, and we'll have to take the pain out. It'll happen when we can feel the pain ourselves, when our pain grows so great that it's no longer our own, when it stops being selfish. But you can't understand these things yet."

Leena was bubbling with thoughts. She'd already forgotten the stone and bird but she remembered she'd heard something from Filemon that made her hurt.

"What does it mean there's no such thing as Leena's matters? That's what Filemon said." Leena looked moody and wronged.

Elisabet sighed. It seemed there was no end to the questions.

"It just means that God keeps you in his breast pocket. Everything's planned ahead of time, everything's actually already happened, that means your fate, too, and so you don't really have a will of your own. When you understand that, you'll also understand that nothing bad can really touch you."

Leena looked helplessly disappointed, like she'd gotten a present or a promise she had no use for.

"But someday you'll understand," Elisabet assured her with a smile. "Actually you do already. Since you dream and play, you know very well—better than I do—that everything's just parallel realities, metaphors. To know that helps you."

But to know that didn't help at all.

"Parallel realities? What does that mean?"

"Just that everything's make believe. That's what it means."

Leena nodded enthusiastically. Now she understood.

"A little like a fairy tale," she said uncertainly—of course she had to prove that she had understood.

"That's right, a little like a fairy tale. Or a little like music. Both make us feel that even if we're here now, within our own narrow boundaries, we're somewhere else in a more whole and personal—more *real*—way."

"Somewhere else . . ." Leena repeated and got a dreamy look in her eye. She vaguely felt she was close to a secret now.

"You seem to think a lot about somewhere else," said Elisabet, noticing she had made an impression on the girl. "What are you thinking about—tell me!"

Leena wasn't thinking of anything but she readily grabbed her chance and immediately started thinking.

"I . . . I once died in water. Make-believe died."

It felt good to get it off her chest. She hadn't dared tell any stranger about her death yet.

"Died? When?"

Leena strained her memory.

"It wasn't long ago. It was when I came down with the falling sickness."

"Came down . . . You have the falling sickness?"

"Yes, or who knows, really, says Grandma. It might be a nicer disease, she says. Though I think the falling sickness is nice enough. It's the same as pepilepsy, and that's Latin."

Elisabet almost laughed. She didn't seem to believe Leena's stories.

"How did you die in water, tell me!"

"The water turned into Heaven and I fell into that Heaven and died. And then the doctor or Jesus woke me up from death and I was in bed and the wallpaper was singing."

"The wallpaper?"

"Yes, or the birds painted on it. They were singing my own songs, and I thought I was in Heaven."

"So you hear voices?"

"No, music. Music and other playing. But I don't always hear it, even if I wanted to."

"Can't you control that music at all, then? I mean can't you lure it to come?"

"Uh-uh. The music comes when it wants to, usually in a dark room, almost in secret. Sometimes you have to lie still and pretend you're not there so the music won't be scared and run away. But some—" Leena drew breath, she wasn't used to speaking for so long at once. "Sometimes it doesn't want to run away, and then it's everywhere."

"The music?"

"Yes. And everything sings." Leena looked thoughtful. Then she said, shyly and yearningly as if declaring her love:

"Grandma's ladle can sing, too."

"Really? That's so nice! I'd give anything if my ladle could sing. There's nothing bad or frightening about hearing music. It's very charming. And I don't think it's strange at all if someone like you sometimes dies in water or falls to Heaven. It's just . . . normal. At your age anything's normal." Elisabet gave a sigh of relief when she came upon such a practical, general word. "You don't really believe you have the falling sickness, do you?"

"I don't know," answered Leena evasively. She was fond of her mysterious disease that had once allowed her to stay home from school. Who knew what liberties it would bring her yet. However, to please Sister Elisabet she said:

"But Grandma doesn't believe in it, she's just scared."

At that moment she remembered she had no business being there so she added, startled:

"I must go now, because Grandma's . . . scared."

"Of course, but you won't be scared anymore—will you? You don't need to have the falling sickness just because Grandma's ladle can sing, right? Of course it can sing, and the main thing is, don't lose your music, Leena. Don't be afraid—and don't forget that everything's just make believe!"

When Elisabet was finished, Leena curtsied. She didn't remember that everything was just make believe so she tried to curtsy like a very good girl, and probably because of that it turned out so clumsy and embarrassing.

AND THEN SHE LEFT, in a daze. Squeezing her ball she slowly backed up to the street; Sister Elisabet waved and smiled her good-byes, and then the smile was left behind the maple leaves.

When she got to the street, Leena realized she hadn't smiled at all herself; she had been too shy and nervous to be able to smile, and that made her feel sorry. So she made her lips smile now that she was walking downhill, even if it was already too late. Leena regretted her slowness but comforted herself by thinking that maybe Elisabet understood, understood that this was what she was like—always a little late. Now her belated smile reached an old woman swaying uphill. Where do I put my smile now? Leena worried, and her lips kept smiling against her will. But the old lady's eyes cast her a friendly glimmer so she didn't care to hide her smile anymore. And many people came her way, and she smiled generously at everyone, and almost everybody she met reflected some of her smile.

When she reached her home yard, she saw that the wonderful evening light that had streamed into the churchyard, seemingly from some other world, liked it here, too. It also liked it in their small home. The simple white bedroom furniture was made strangely luminous and almost transparent by a rosy hue; it looked like these ethereal objects might drift away at any moment and disappear like spirits into the surrounding light.

Leena looked around, fascinated. She felt like she had been away from home for a very long time and returned a changed person. Her home had changed, too: the sorrow that used to dwell there was gone. There was just warmth and light and a strange static waiting.

Leena tiptoed around the room, caressing everything as if she wanted to feel that it really existed. These old acquaintances, whose every feature she knew by heart, now moved her wonderfully. She loved them all, loved in the wistful way you love a friend who's been lost and found again.

"The Lord is my shepherd; I shall not want. Psalm 23."

The Bible verse embroidered in inept, clumsy cursive on a piece of linen had felt so imposing to her; because of its constant presence its gospel had started to bore and bother her, but now it suddenly awoke new feelings of happiness and trust. Suddenly it occurred to her that the sentence blossoming on the wall of her house on its own accord, quite indifferent to any ill feeling on her part, really contained all she needed to know; and should she embrace this knowledge, she'd really want for nothing.

Shh, shh, shepherd. The Lord is my shh-shh-shepherd; I shall not want. Yes, of course, that way it was even more beautiful. Like a lullaby. If you looked and listened for a while, it turned into music. What was it that was playing so beautifully? Must be love playing, Leena thought suddenly. Hush, my love—shh, shh.

And so she became familiar with universal love for the first time through the Bible verse embroidered in such an awkward, and thus moving, way. She didn't know what it was and where it came from, but suddenly she realized she wasn't without love; it was mysteriously all around her, just like the air she breathed.

Grandma had always loved her, of course. But Grandma's love walked in black, it was as gloomy and sorrowful as her hymns. Besides, it wasn't a gift but somehow automatic. It was part of the household, Leena was quick to think. She immediately felt bad and regretted her thought deeply.

Pained by a feeling of guilt, she remembered Grandma's wrinkled face, worn almost transparent by endless worrying, her eyes paled by sorrow, the eyes that couldn't cry. But now that she in her mind's eye tried to see Grandma's face clearly, she realized in confusion that she couldn't remember it. It was like trying to draw in water: the lines trembled and broke, and the mirror emptied. Halfway between real and unreal wavered a shadow so thin and fragile the wind could have blown straight through it. That was Grandma.

Grandma . . . Now she felt a tender ache for the mere word. Grandma—where was she now? In the kitchen? No—she wasn't there, either. And yet there was someone there: the same lingering silence that was everywhere, its presence so strangely alive that she could almost hear it breathe.

Leena then realized that Grandma had noticed her disappearance and gone to look for her. So she guessed she in turn had to go looking for Grandma. Where to look, she had no idea, but she left promptly and in good faith: you'll find your way when you're doing the right thing.

She hadn't wandered for long before she found herself on the seaside at the opposite edge of town, on the same banks from where she had once been carried home, unconscious. It had taken her this long to remember that she wasn't allowed to wander off by herself; still, her feet wanted to walk on the bridge, they wanted to hear the bridge echo under them, and she couldn't disobey them. The bridge was the most exciting place in the whole town; it was exhilarating to think that when she walked on the bridge, she was actually walking on water. Jesus had walked on water like this, too, except there was no bridge there. Then she started running and pretended to be a horse. Horses must love crossing the bridge like this—drum-dee-dum, the sound resounded along the shoreline. For a moment she wondered whether she'd rather be a horse than Leena, but then the bridge ended and she remembered Elisabet and Filemon and Bach, and that she, too, would learn to play the music that had God in it. And so she accepted her own self fully and without condition.

And when she looked at the reeds growing by the bridge, she saw that they were shaped just like organ pipes, and the water's soft, slim fingers played them, just like it wanted to copy Bach.

Then she noticed some cow parsley by the reeds and realized that she wanted to copy Bach, too. She should probably practice a little now that she'd soon be a real musician. And she broke off a good piece of the stem, and there was her flute.

Very pleased with her instrument, Leena ran back to the bridge and started to blow with all her heart. The whistle gave a pleasant hiss, and in Leena's ears it was full of music. The cow parsley sang, the girl's heart sang, and she even made up lyrics in her mind.

A lil' flute,
Not a lute,
Played shrill-shrill-shrill-lil-lil-ly.
On the bridge,
High pitch,
Played that lil' flute shrill-lil-ly.

It was the hymn of the Flute, at the same time happy and sad and very, very dreamy. Then Leena again remembered the church and Bach, and a destructive doubt crept into her heart. Her music wouldn't be good enough for church; maybe it wasn't good enough for God, either. What good was her playing if there was no God in her music? Or was there? Maybe God only accepted Bach who had been dead for two hundred years.

And an unspeakable distress and concern filled the soul so fond of its own song. Leena, feeling down, was wondering whether God would accept her music at all, whether God could dream—just a little, just enough to understand the cow parsley flute that dreamed so whole-heartedly.

And suddenly she knew: it was certain God could dream—God could do anything. If he just had the *time* to listen to Leena's music, he surely didn't much care what sort of whistle Leena played, as long as the playing was beautiful.

So she gave up the bothersome worrying, solemnly

leaned against the railing and started composing with renewed faith.

And the cow parsley flute wept and laughed, almost out of breath, and Leena had no idea where her magic music came from. And when the tunes dropped into the water, rings appeared and spread endlessly and listened to her playing.

And the water dimmed and the wind slept and somewhere far away there was an invisible line where the sea leaked into the sky. The water was listening to her, and the wind was listening to her, and her heart went still, time after time, as it listened to the music leaking into the sky.

"Hey, girl, how can you make a sound with such a puny little whistle?"

It was a stranger, an odd passerby who just needed to hear his own voice, because having spoken he went away, sniggering. But that was all it took to scare Leena. The flute fell from her hands, the music dropped through her fingers, fell into the water, and drowned.

And just then she saw that the night was dark and the banks eerie and deserted. All the stars had rained down from the sky, and darkness blanketed the water like a heavy weight.

And she stood alone by the dead waters and mourned her music like she'd lost it forever.

SHE HAD WALKED for a long time when a slow drizzle started. She came to a boulevard of tall, gloomy trees. She could smell the earth and decomposing leaves, the scent of impermanence. The shadows of the trees rustled softly on the dark pavement, and the rain gently veiled her. Then she began to watch her own shadow following her up one street, down another, and she felt an indistinct happiness about the fact that it followed her around, that it stopped when she stopped; when she hurried on, so did her shadow. It was somehow a comfort that this silent companion ran after her, wanted to go where she went, wanted to show her that it was she who was walking here, Saara Magdaleena Muisto Susanna, and nobody else.

When she came to her own gate, the streetlight went on above her head—but she didn't notice that. She only noticed that the shadow suddenly disappeared, vanished from existence, and a new, destructive terror sneaked into her mind: she felt like she herself had ceased to exist, dissolved into the rain along with her shadow.

How it happened, she couldn't quite understand; she only felt that her existence ceased in some horrible, incomplete way, that she dissolved in water, earth, rain, the decomposing leaves and flickering shadows, everywhere and nowhere.

She didn't know how she got home; suddenly she just found herself in the kitchen, and there was an emptiness, a silence in and around her.

Leena's wildly squinting eyes scared Grandma, who immediately brought her drops from the cupboard. The medicine called Devil's dung was bitter like sin, but the girl swallowed it without batting an eye. She seemed to hardly taste anything out of the ordinary. Mechanically she started slurping the tea Grandma had poured her, and mechanically she answered Grandma's pained questions. She knew that Grandma had been frantically searching for her, but the worry didn't really reach her—after all, she didn't exist. She drank her tea and accounted for her adventures in detail, and still she didn't exist.

Then she heard Grandma say she wasn't allowed to go to the Roman Catholic Church on Vesiportinkatu anymore. Grandma's ban didn't make her feel bad; Vesiportinkatu seemed to her as unreal as a dream or a faded picture she had looked at a long time ago. Maybe she'd never even been there. Everything seemed oddly inconsequential and strange: she was absolutely outside of things, she'd fallen

off, ceased to exist. Still, she heard her mouth say that
Vesiportinkatu was the most beautiful fairy-tale street in
the whole world and that Sister Elisabet was as sweet as
an angel.

"But she has a foreign religion, and you're not allowed
to go there anymore."

Leena thought to herself that all angels must have a foreign religion in that case, but she didn't know what foreign
meant exactly, so she said:

"She's an angel anyway."

"You're a silly one. Those Catholics know how to pose
as angels when they want to seduce folks to the shelter of
their misguided church."

What folks? Leena thought to herself. But she still
thought that Grandma probably knew what she was talking
about, so she had nothing more to say. She didn't distin-
guish between right and wrong, just beautiful and ugly.
Sister Elisabet's church was beautiful. Not that the church
that she and Grandma sometimes went to wasn't, but it was
too big and public, official like a school. It wouldn't have
been okay to drop the ball there. If she'd done that there,
she'd surely go to hell when she died. And there was no
flour sack that thought it was a dog, or vice versa. And no
Filemon who was a little odd and a little drunk, but other
than that nice and very funny.

As she thus protested to herself, the emptiness and horror started to fade, and she felt a bit better. So she tried once again:

"And Elisabet promised to teach me to play music with Filemon."

"Play music, you? You who can't even eat your porridge without spilling it. A musician! It's not fitting work for decent people. Your father was a no-good musician and that's caused us enough trouble as it is. Music's no use, really—you go to bed at once."

Grandma's words hurt Leena's feelings, and she decided to hate everything useful from then on. Grandma talked about music like it was porridge or potatoes: "Music is not even edible." Leena felt almost dirty, ripped her clothes off spitefully and crawled into bed full of dull gloom.

"Would you like anything?" asked Grandma, her voice gentle and remorseful. "Maybe some raisins, the ones that Eevertti Anselmi sent."

Leena shook her head. She didn't want anything—not anymore, now that her music had dissolved in the water and her shadow had dissolved in rain and even music tasted of oatmeal.

Then she tried thinking that her shadow had gone to get the music from the water but even she herself couldn't believe in her own fairy tale. And she turned towards the wall and stared at the wallpaper and the birds on it, the dead birds who would never again sing to her.

And she stared and stared until they dimmed and vanished in the mist that rose from the forest surrounding them.

Then a bird crawled out of her ear and fluttered off; ten, a hundred, a thousand birds crawled out of her ear, and they all flew away. But the last bird stayed with her and grew and grew until she couldn't see the end of its tail. And it looked at her with its round red eyes and ate her up.

And next she knew she was that bird herself. And she spread her wings and flew towards the red ball that took on the glimmer of the sun. And apart from herself and the sun, there was nothing but silence.

Then the sun exploded and fell away and disappeared. After the sun, a wonderful music came on and she flew along with it.

And on the music walked Bach, who resembled a penguin like Sister Elisabet and carried Filemon's pumpkin in his arms. And she sang the songs of the cow parsley whistle to Bach, and Bach smiled and clapped his hands. And she smiled, too, and her smile was right on time.

She awoke to a feeling of ecstatic happiness, and when she opened her eyes, Bach had turned into a table lamp. Grandma was sitting by the lamp peering at the Bible;

her eyeglasses had slipped down her nose and were almost falling off, her knobby finger traveled slowly back and forth across the tobacco-brown page of the old book as she read in a shaky voice:

"Verily, verily, I say unto thee, except a man be born of water and of the Spirit, he cannot enter into the kingdom of God. The wind bloweth where it listeth, and thou hearest the sound thereof, but canst not tell whence it cometh, and whither it goeth: so is everyone that is born of the Spirit."

"Grandma . . ."

"Yes?"

"How do you explain dreams? Where did you learn?"

"Dreams are a vessel of prophecy, and those blessed with a long life of almost a hundred years know how to interpret dreams, too."

"What's prophecy?"

"Oh . . . That's a way of reading forebodings, almost like soothsaying—in a Christian, God-fearing way."

"What are forebodings?"

"There are many kinds. There's dreaming, revelations, and other signs God gives the weak in spirit to announce himself. 'I will open my mouth in parables; I will utter things which have been kept secret from the foundation of the world,' says the Lord."

"Parables? Is that the same as metaphor?"

"It's the same."

Leena thought of Sister Elisabet's teachings and said confidently:

"A metaphor . . . that's the same as make believe. God's playing when he utters secret things like that—in parables."

"Huh? God doesn't play, but announces himself in advance, for everything will happen just like it's been written."

"And it's all make believe. Everything's just make believe," Leena testified.

"What are you saying . . . Have you learned that light-headed lesson from that place on Vesiportinkatu? That God's playing make believe?"

"Yes, or . . . God, in a way . . . composes, I mean."

"Well, they've composed one funny religion in your head. God isn't playing but warning us. Now tell me your dream if you've been shown dreams."

So Leena told her. She spoke her dream out loud, thoroughly, and her words were followed by a deep silence. When she looked questioningly at Grandma, she realized that Grandma's feelings were hurt and she was crying, that her very essence was crying silently. And Leena didn't understand, because she had thought the bird dream was heavenly and beautiful.

Then Grandma got up and went to lean on the tile

stove like she wanted to get warm or support herself on it. She had on her black blouse and the shiny, silky skirt, with long hems that touched the floor; the skirt was older than Leena. Leena remembered hearing that the skirt had been made in honor of Grandpa, who a long time ago had hanged himself from the flue chain. Since then their stoves had no more flue chains and Grandma had no more tears. Grandma's eyes are drier than her eyeglasses, yet she's crying—a soundless, horrible crying that can't express itself.

She's crying even now. A cry like that could kill a person, it occurs to Leena, and she's blown away by a terrible panic. She has looked at Grandma a thousand times but just now sees her for the first time. Grandma's exactly the same as always, faded, gray, dressed in black, and still more alive than ever. She's no longer the paper cutting that is transparent when you look at it against the light. And she's no longer to be taken for granted, forever there. She's a living person, too alive, so terribly alive that she might die of it.

Until now Leena has thought of her grandma as something that's existed from the beginning of time and will exist till the end of the world. It was a nice and practical way of seeing it. Grandma has endured like some rare plant that has been pressed and dried and glued on white paper; this white paper stood for Leena's life. But now this picture was no longer true. Nothing permanent was true anymore—nothing was certain.

But the terrible thing couldn't happen. It was her business to stop it at any cost. Once Eevertti got there, they'd figure out a way, a trick that would guarantee certainty for Grandma—not for all eternity but close enough. Till then Leena should fatten her up, because Grandma ate so little. From now on Leena would make sure she wouldn't just nibble at her food but ate heartily. Oh, and drank lots of Devil's dung and eau-de-vie to boot.

Leena found peace for her soul in good faith and conviction and fell into the lake of sleep.

THEN CAME MONDAY and the evening of detention. Leena didn't want to tell Grandma about the theft, the reason for detention, to keep her from dying of sorrow—but made up a very innocent story about half the class being punished for a badly learned lesson. Even crime took loyalty, so Leena was making progress in the difficult art of lying.

The evening was rainy and miserable; even the sky took part in her lowly, sad state. When she got out the door, into the yard, she stepped right in a puddle. Shivering, she shoved her hands deeper into her pockets and started reluctantly across the yard. She felt her shame turning into tears and rolling down her cheeks, but she didn't care; she just let the rain mix its own sweeter pearls into hers.

Then she noticed what a nice song the rain made in her shoes and was distracted by listening. It purled and gurgled and spoke her name in the shoe. It was almost funny. She plodded the wet streets without looking around, the rain's lulling trickle in her ears, the shoe singing.

Then she got near the school, and the shoe sang to a slower rhythm. At the corner near the school there was a linden, and it shook drops of water down Leena's neck. Leena was soaked and miserable and would rather have died, somewhere there among the fallen leaves.

But her feet took her mechanically to the deserted schoolyard, to the janitor's door. The hesitant, rusty sound of the doorbell summoned the wife of the janitor, "Kapteenska," to the door.

"Leena—just look at you! What are you doing here—at this hour?" The friendly, round face was full of astonishment.

Leena was shivering, humiliated, and cold, and couldn't get a word out of her mouth.

"Look at you—all wet—come in, hurry now!"

Leena made herself enter, miserable; she noticed the inviting smell of onions and frying fat.

"Well, what can we do for you?" tries the janitor's wife again.

"She told me to . . . The teacher, I mean . . ." Leena mumbles.

"Jesus, Mary, and Joseph—detention? In this God-awful rain, like the Heavenly Father was out to drown all his critters."

Kapteenska's babbling sounds comforting to Leena and

goes well with the smell of fried meat. She takes off her dripping jacket and her shame, too, and follows Kapteenska along the dark corridors of the school building. She falls into the darkness like into a well, and the horror takes over again. Kapteenska swaggers like a small leprechaun ahead of her, her steps echoing hollowly on the stone corridors that seem to never end. And suddenly Leena feels that there's no reason for her to be in this dead, dark building, she's here by accident and everything's a mistake—everything.

Still, here she is—here she is walking automatically, by mistake, by mere chance. The walls push towards her, the stairs slip away from under her feet, and the echo nails her steps on the walls. She walks like in a nightmare and is already sure that this going will never end—the stairs, corridor, darkness—the horrible circle built of stone and the dark she must encircle forever.

At last the stairs end, however, and the terrible spell is broken. Kapteenska turns the switch, and a piercing brightness explodes into the corridor. The key squeaks in the lock, the classroom door opens with a cry and another light goes on, a thin, hooded light on the teacher's desk.

"Find your desk, now, and sit down," says Kapteenska in her ordinary voice that sounds too familiar inside these forbidding walls. "Guess your teacher'll be here soon."

The door closes and Leena is left alone. She sinks into

her chair and stares at the ink-stained desktop in a muddled frame of mind. Suddenly she feels a deep fondness
for the shapeless stain. She has made it, she's identified
the torturous place, marked the desk forever. She's had
to suffer humiliation and shame for it, but the mark will
last, no matter what. It has eaten into the wood and will
endure. When she leaves here, there'll be a mark, the dark
trace of her accident that signifies her. It's part of her, in a
rather mysterious way it is a part of her: the frozen horror,
the cry from her mouth.

Instinctively she understands that the dried black puddle on the desk contains a secret promise, the magic of
atonement. The puddle has turned into a map, the map of
her Via Dolorosa, which tells the story of what she once had
to endure in front of this neat and hated desk. Someone
had wounded her, and out of the wound bubbled black ink
onto the desk.

For a long time she has wallowed in the mystery of blood
and ink, in the good teachings of passion and redemption
that have begun to dawn on her there, by the profound
marks of the old sin. There's no more shame, nor a stain;
the stain has blossomed like a rose, atoned the torment and
the hardship and elevated it to the realm of eternal gems.

Outside, the rain's dripping past the windows inces-
santly, and like the rain, time's dripping out. Desks swim

in greenish light like islands, and nine metallic clangs pulse in that light. Leena wakes. It's nine o'clock, and the teacher hasn't come yet. Surely she won't come now. She lied—or she simply forgot, Leena adds to herself, generously. Could she leave, maybe? Dare she? At least she dares go to the window to see whether the teacher is coming.

Deep in thought, she wades among the desks and through the water-colored light to the window, climbs onto the window sill and presses her nose against the pane. Behind the window the rain is streaming down relentlessly, and the gutter makes strings of pearls out of the droplets and transforms them into music. The melodies chase each other, skip down invisible stairs endlessly, endlessly—like that one time in Sister Elisabet's church. The fugue—the fugue was like this, Leena remembers. The rain has composed a fugue for the gutters, almost as skillfully as Father Bach.

The rain doesn't tire of playing, and Leena doesn't tire of listening. The wet asphalt glimmers on the ground, and the rain splatters onto the street so furiously that the drops bounce back and turn into glittering mist. It looks like the rain is coming up from the street. Just below her floats a yellow lantern, drawing a dim circle into the rain. Then she notices a big lone umbrella swinging slowly under the street light. It's red like a fly agaric and walking in the rain all by itself. Maybe it really thinks it's a fly agaric and goes to the forest to make tiny baby mushrooms.

Leena looks lovingly at the umbrella walking in the street, and suddenly she comes up with a new reason for excitement: she now knows what to ask Eevertti Anselmi for a present. She'll ask for an umbrella. A big purple silk umbrella to glimmer and sing in the rain . . . And when a windy day comes, she'll spread the umbrella like wings and fly. She wants an umbrella—wings, wings.

And she decides to write to Eevertti at once, write a very fine, civilized letter. She can borrow some civilization from Sister Elisabet's teachings, she thinks practically; for the letter must be impressive. She gets her writing things from her desk, and excitedly she starts writing. The language yields to her laboring mind and hand, and she has to rewrite her message many times before she's happy with it. Finally she gives it the last touch and writes the final draft with solemn, wavering letters:

Dear Eevertti Anselmi!!!

I met Elisabet and Filemon who's all blind but still knows Bakh by heart. He has a pipe and a beard and a pumpkin who's a dog and he's really sad, and that's why he sometimes drinks too much wine with a tender heart and gets wings for his wretched soul. Then he's very funny and nicely Hilarious. And I'd like wings, too, because I'm so sad here on earth and have a Wretched Soul. Wings, Dear Uncle Eevertti Anselmi, wings meaning Umbrella. Purple and very big, the biggest there is. So you can fly with it. And it should be silk, see-through silk so that under it you can clearly hear how the rain plays copying Bakh who died 200 years ago. Dear Uncle Eevertti Anselmi, please send me wings!

Best wishes, Leena

Leena had just finished her letter when the door opened and the janitor's wife came into the classroom with her arms crossed.

"Looks like the teacher's not coming," she said. "Musta forgotten all about detention—who knows, but that's what it looks like. You go on home now, poor girl—I'll testify you been here the whole time."

Leena didn't need to be told twice. She quickly gathered her papers, gave Kapteenska a quick curtsy and danced down the stairs.

The next few days Leena lived in a dream. At school she sometimes awoke to the teacher telling her to get up so that she could interrogate her, but she answered the questions automatically, without losing heart, and soon fell back to the atmosphere of happy waiting. Neither the school nor anything else could ruin this atmosphere; besides, school didn't seem half as important as before, and even the teacher wasn't as scary anymore. If the teacher was angry, it must be the rules, Leena thought magnanimously. You had to be angry if you were paid for it. And to her knowledge the teacher was paid. Leena didn't care to think about it anymore, she was busy waiting for her umbrella. Her dream about the umbrella was so perfect that she was almost as happy as if she already owned the umbrella. And since she was happy, she could afford to be tolerant and generous towards the school, too.

And when the dream turned into reality, it didn't vanish like dreams usually do, since it still half-belonged to the realms of imagination. She was handed the dream—big, purple, bright—and it didn't vanish. She stroked the umbrella's translucent silk and smiled to herself in bliss.

Wings—she had gotten wings.

And nothing was lacking in her happiness—nothing but a bit of rain.

But the rain didn't come that day or the next. Those days Leena spent most of her time in the corner of the bedroom, under the umbrella, reading books and thinking about the secret wisdom of fairy tales. And the dreams of the books became so real to her that she couldn't separate those everlasting dreams from her own anymore. In a country unbelievably far away, in a country that might not even exist, she picked stinging nettle at grave sites, and with burning fingers she weaved armor for her bird brothers out of the nettle, to free them from a terrible spell. Was it possible, she thought frantically, almost feeling the pain for real. Of course the impossible was possible. And it happened. If Leena believed she was the Eliisa of the fairy tale, Eliisa of the fairy tale believed she was Leena, and the fairy tale happened just like it was written.

And Leena was happy. She was happy even waiting for rain, and soon her happy expectation was rewarded. The sky was cloudy and gray with rain one chilly morning in late October, and when Leena had her clothes on and books packed in her knapsack, the first drops fell onto the window. She snatched the umbrella and ran out in the yard without drinking her tea. This way she stole enough time to go to school by the big boulevard.

When she spread the umbrella outside the door, she felt she had spread her wings, wide, shiny, and strong. The wind made the silk rustle like wings taking flight. A boundless joy hummed through her as the wind grabbed the glittery silk and pushed her and the umbrella across the yard like a kite. When she slowed her step on the street, the gust was tired of the game and the rain pitter-pattered rhythmically on top of her head. It was music in Leena's ears, bittersweet, lovely music. The rain composed a waltz for the umbrella, and for want of something better Leena borrowed the lyrics of her old favorite song:

> The years have gone by,
> The bird cherry perfume—
> Youth has long ago passed us by . . .

Like that. The rain moves like that, and just like that she makes her way along the sidewalk. Dances. Dances with the umbrella, a waltz, and youth has long ago passed her by. The umbrella is her partner and leads her in the waltz—just like that! Like that it bows and leads her, leads her through the whole town. And the town's dancing, too. The whole world's dancing. World . . . The world is a silky half-globe going around—going round and round with her waltz. And her partner bowing and leading.

The bird cherry perfume . . .

Dizzying. Dizzying. Leena is dizzy with happiness, so is the umbrella, so is the world.

Going round and round, the world going round until it's dizzy with the umbrella waltz. Around the waltz, around itself, the world spinning drunkenly around Leena—like that.

Youth has long ago . . .

The world's singing, the world's dancing, the world is beautiful and mad with happiness.

Passed us by . . .

But the world is beautiful only as long as school isn't in it. Just like that the umbrella partner's neck stiffens, it stops bowing and leading. The waltz stops going around and the world squeaks to a stop. Leena is close to the school, and the whole world stops and turns shadowy. Her steps become hesitant and she tries to slip deeper under the umbrella.

Then she awakes to an odd silence: the schoolyard is empty, taken over by an awful silence. She's late, and the sin of lateness means reproach and public humiliation. The teacher will interrogate her like a criminal, write complaints to Grandma and make her stand in the corner pondering the misery of life. And the umbrella will have to stand in the corner and think about the misery of life, too, in the corner of the gallows hall, accompanied by galoshes. Her purple, blissful umbrella that loves the rain and wants to dance and fly . . . No, she won't go to school, ever again. She'll go to Old Town and show the umbrella the street that falls to Heaven. And then she'll go to Elisabet. The Almost-Mom, Pretend Mom, Angel Mom.

The ugly school is left behind; she's happy again, in the rain, in the music, in the idea of Angel Mom. Up the street, down the other sidewalk, the girl, her shadow, and her reflection, a threesome blessedly in love. The world is grand and beautiful again, this purple world of hers. Like a great flower, bloomed from a dream, it shines above her, sways in the asphalt mirror beneath her feet, bursts into music and song, and glimmers. In every puddle on her way blooms a purple flower, the rain sprinkles silver laughter, and the asphalt blossoms and sings. The asphalt is all translucent underneath her, made of glass, and that's why it makes music. And she has wings, wings that rustle softly, sweeping her through this musical world made of purple glass. She flies, flies to Heaven Street, to Angel Mom who will teach her to play, too.

Now they're there, the girl and the umbrella; it's hard to see the little vagabond under the umbrella at all. But she is bursting with happiness; hardly ever has one umbrella sheltered so much happiness. At least Leena herself believes that the greatest happiness in the world has been collected under the most beautiful umbrella in the world—under the wings, under the wings, yes.

The sand on the maple-lined path shines damp with rain; it looks like pearls have been scattered in her way. At the end of the road glimmers the white church through the rain; it glimmers like an underwater temple with shimmering outlines, and Leena thinks it's like a seashell where God's music hums, and she's on her way there, on her way into the seashell.

She stops on the stairs, confused. A large sheet of white paper is nailed on the church door, something was penciled on it but the rain has washed the writing out. The letters have run in rivulets to the bottom edge of the paper, there's just some faded curl of a cursive letter left, and Leena can't make out any whole words.

A strange anxiety, a bad feeling, overwhelms her. She feels like she's received a very important letter she can't read. Distressed, she grabs the door handle with both hands, but the door won't open. The door is as taciturn and mute as the message she can't read. It's in front of her, as unmovable as a rock, and no knocking or command will open the bolts.

Her hands, turning blue with the cold, freeze around

the metal handle, but she's not feeling the cold, not understanding the passage of time. She only understands the aggressive obstinacy of the door. The door is big, gloomy, and expressionless, like it's decided for itself never to open again.

Finally she gives up her futile struggle and turns away from the stairs, exhausted. Mechanically she lifts the umbrella from a step and wanders mindlessly back to the street.

The world of Bach and Sister Elisabet has disappeared. Since time doesn't exist to her, since there's only the present, it's gone from her forever.

The girl and the umbrella wander resignedly up one street, down the other. Even the miracle of the wings has been killed now. Maybe she had flown too far, flown till she had exhausted herself. The wings have withered and can't carry her anymore.

And still she's moving, even without the wings she's moving. She's now empty, and that's why she moves with a strange lightness. And suddenly everything feels strangely meaningless and good. It feels good to think that nothing more will happen, that she doesn't need to expect anything anymore. How did Sister Elisabet put it? "Everything's actually already happened, that means your fate, too." That everything has happened, it means that everything is in the past, that there's really nothing. *Nothing.* She knows that now in her heart.

There's nothing, not even her, no Leena. There's only a thought that once went to a little church to hear God's music. And the Mother of God stepped down from her golden frame, came to her and introduced herself as Sister Elisabet. And then Mother of God—Angel Mom, Pretend-Mom—opened her eyes and showed her there's nothing.

There's only music, the living water God's finger writes in. Everything else is misunderstanding and delusion. But people don't know that, so they're unhappy.

But Leena knows, somewhere beyond consciousness she knows everything, and she's no longer unhappy. An unnaturally clear, redeeming knowledge—God's music, water, nothing—has hummed through her, and now she feels a strange clarity and coolness. Wonderfully lightly, weightlessly she walks through the weightless world. She's wandered in a long nightmare's maze, but now she's stepped out of the dream, and the horrible spell is broken. She's outside everything, and nothing can hurt her anymore. She's outside herself, but not alone. Her own wings no longer carry her; someone else is carrying her.

Someone's carrying her, someone unknown and mighty. She only needs to go where she's taken. There's nothing other than this new wonderful certainty. She's not thinking of anything, but she *knows*—knows like a fallen leaf God blows on.

A leaf—fallen off a fairy tale. Has she fallen off some fairy tale? Didn't she once, a long time ago, read a dangerously beautiful fairy tale that was written about her? It was a bad fairy tale and she was very afraid. But she's not afraid anymore. Life's no longer a bad fairy tale, it's just a fairy tale, sweetly inconsequential. And she's not curious to see how it ends.

When she comes to the bridge by the shore, where she died in the water the first time, the rain has stopped and the sky is like a gigantic silk umbrella, translucent and full of invisible light. The day is slowly dying, and on the far horizon shines a red ball, the coppery autumn sun that's about to step down into the sea. Leena is sitting on the old boat pier and floating an imaginary bark boat, mirages looming in her eyes.

Here there's a silence where a weary wind sleeps, and strange trees that sway in still air. All birds have turned into fishes and gone quiet, but their songs are safe, all the songs of the earth and water and air are safe, shut up in boxes made of seashells, on the sea bottom. There's the music and the secret and all God's writings.

"The main thing is, don't you lose your music, Leena."

Leena looks around her, surprised; she's heard Sister Elisabet's voice clearly. But the shore is empty and motionless, only the clouds glide by her as silently as thoughts.

She remembers again the miracles of her Sunday revelation: the bottomless gaze of the Madonna with the pigeon and the music that came over her in waves like eternity. And the old, boundless longing and mourning for her own music take over.

How could she lose her music and drop it in the water? She stood right there on the bridge, a stone's throw away from the pier, blowing her flute, blowing it like she was born with a whistle for a beak. And then came the man, and the whistle fell and was lost.

And the music . . . For the whistle wasn't any ordinary songbird, even if it was just a piece of cow parsley: Father Bach in the clouds had given it its song. And she had blundered and lost this heavenly instrument.

"The main thing is, don't lose your music, Leena."

Again—she was speaking again—Elisabet who didn't exist. Or did she? *Yes*. Now she saw the light. She saw the light somewhere deep inside. Elisabet existed because the dream existed. Only dreams are real, not people. Only the dream is real, everything else is just gray.

And that's why she has to get her music back. Somehow

she must find it again, she can't abandon her music. She must save her enchanted flute, she *must*.

But how . . . Deep in thought, she descends the steps at the end of the pier and sits on the last step and starts drawing circles in the water. She draws on the water and the clouds, gliding like ships under her feet. She draws on the sides of the ships.

LEENA. She named a ship after herself. Its sails swelled up, slowly and grandly it left the pier and drifted away. It looked almost self-conscious as it continued its sea journey. As it should be, since it wasn't just any ship anymore, it was a christened and ceremonially launched ship, a ship that knew something.

Ship that knew . . . Right then a happy thought takes off, like a bird from its nest. Now she knows—knows how to get her flute back.

She does have a boat: her gigantic umbrella. She'll row out to retrieve her music.

But she has to hurry, she must leave right away if she wants to get her music back. The music can escape with the wind or the current and sail all the way to America. She can't be a moment late, or else everything is lost.

With impatient hands, full of the restlessness of leaving, she opens the umbrella and launches it into the sea, watches for a while its innocent, fascinating sway and quickly takes off her knapsack and jacket. Then she grasps tightly the last step from the pier and in awe she takes a step into the shining vessel.

LEENA FEELS AN ODD, sharp pain, the same as when she woke up to the singing of the birds on the wallpaper and found the robed doctor by her bedside. Now the birds aren't singing, though, and around her there's an emptiness full of silence and darkness. It must be nighttime and she should be sleeping, that's the rule. She squeezes her eyes shut and tries to lure sleep to come. But sleep doesn't come, and the strange pain is keeping her awake.

To pass the time she tries to remember yesterday and make pictures of it like she was building a jigsaw puzzle, but she's lost all the pieces, lost yesterday, and can't remember anything. Yesterday? It feels like a really long time has passed, a thousand years or longer, so long she can't even count that far.

What's happened then? She can't remember. Her mind is as blank and dark as the world around her. Then something moves inside her: water. It's happened. Water.

Then she remembers something else, too: the sun had

exploded underwater, and hot, shiny shards were raining around her. And she had picked up a piece of the sun and burned her fingers, burned her fingers in the sun. But right then she realized that it wasn't the sun that had exploded, but her head. Her head had exploded and the hot shards rained hissing down around her.

Leena tries her head, and it's still there. Of course, all that was naturally a dream, things like that happen in dreams, there's nothing strange about that. But her fingers are still burning. Then she remembers that she's knitted shirts for her bird brothers out of nettles and blistered her fingers. That was very long ago too—was it? When was that? In the past? In the future? She can't remember.

Weird, not being able to remember anything. Something funny has happened in her head. Maybe it did explode, after all, and she was given a new head that behaves a bit recklessly and can't remember things. Or she's gotten an alarm clock, a cute one with a shiny case, but strangely forgetful.

Alarm clock, alarm clock, alarm and bell, bell and skull, yes of course, there was talk about that.

Leena listens to hear whether her head is ticking. No, it's not, it's very quiet. Okay, it has to be wound first. When both clock keys are wound, it will ring. She can set it to ring at a certain time and then she'll never be late to school.

Leena is hoping that her bell head can play a waltz. They used to have a clock that could play a waltz for as long as you wanted. It was nice. It would be nice to go to school with a waltzing head.

Yet she feels she probably won't have to go to school anymore. It seems that such bizarre things are happening in her head that she won't have to. They probably don't want a girl whose head looks like an alarm clock and is playing music . . . Well, that's good. She's happy with the alarm clock. It could be quite nice instead of her head, once you get used to it.

But she can't get used to this pain. It's really not that bad but it's strangely all over the place, it's everywhere, in and around her, and it's carrying her, making her move forward and up, towards something unknown.

Making her. Suddenly she notices she's walking within her pain, alone. She also notices it's nighttime, and she's walking through the night, through the dark street. Why is she allowed to walk alone in the middle of the night like this? She's probably walking here without permission. She probably fell asleep somewhere—on the bridge, on the banks, wherever—like once before. Fell to heaven and woke up in the middle of the street and then wandered on half-asleep.

Half-asleep, half-fuddled, foggy, foggy head, there was

nothing strange about that. It happened sometimes when you were deeply tired or even more deeply lost in thought. Lost lost last. Last. Rites. Agony. Then you could fall asleep while standing up or while walking and wake up in a whole new place, to a changed world. It was funny and exciting, almost like moving in a dream. Like now. Moving. Move move move moving. Moving from? No, moving on. The pain pushes on. Maybe it was the funny, exciting sickness that so muddled one up, and the world. Eppy-peppy, or something like that. Odd. Odd nod oddly nodding on and on and on and on—

Her steps echo. The steps echo a-go-go-going on. Her thoughts follow the rhythm of the going, just the going counts, nothing else. Between the thoughts it's dark and empty, and a stunning pain carries her from darkness to darkness.

Suddenly she feels there's something important beyond darkness. Is she looking for something, maybe? She can't remember. Although that's good. Usually you find things you've lost once you've stopped looking. Then finding them is like getting a present. Maybe she'll now be presented with what she's not looking for anymore. She'll find it somewhere suddenly—in a gutter, a crack in a rock, by a water pump, under the tracks. Under the eaves, under the eaves where the wind has gone to sleep.

Sleep, sleep, from dark slumber not a peep.

Sleep peep . . . All her thoughts tangle into a sleepy knot out of spite, they tangle just for fun.

Go to sleep, not a peep, sleep sleep!

Leena feels tired. She wants to creep into sleep in the gutter, in the rainspout, go with the wind. Yes, embrace the wind.

Embrace rainspout
Rainspout drink drunk
Embrace the breeze
In sleepy peace
Embrace—

One empty idea after another lights up on a dark street, flickers a moment and goes out. But her feet wander on all the time, automatically, systematically. And the wind, the wind wanders, too. It hadn't gone to sleep, it had lied. It was plotting something . . . Plotting? A complex plot had been laid out, so she had to walk on and on. Had to walk—careful not to, not to trip. Care dare trip . . . Tangled again. Everything was tangled, and she needed to straighten it out. Everything. Untangle every single thing.

But it was hard. If something was badly tangled, it was hard to untangle. You needed to fiddle with it all day, and you couldn't use scissors. No scissors. Because it wouldn't do to use scissors. You needed to tear, tear and cry though your fingers burned, the nettles burned, the nettles, the knots blistered . . . No scissors. Or it was foul play. Foul play.

Play at, at what—

What? Leena looks up at the sky. She sees a dim lantern above her, swinging slowly in the wind. No, no, it's not a lantern, it's a star, and it's just her head nodding in the wind. The star is not nodding but it softly squeaks, turning on its orbit. Leena stops to listen. Maybe it has something to say, maybe it'll play . . .

And suddenly she hears clearly that it plays a tune, and the melody is scary and bad.

The pain inside her grows and pushes her on. It must have some meaning. What can it be? Where's she going? The pain doesn't say anything, but it forces her on.

Then the star with the bad melody sways off course and starts to whistle. *Vreeew* . . . a hissing arch, and the star is gone. But new stars light up—a hundred, a thousand, a million new stars, the sky is full of stars, and they draw lines and patterns that have some meaning. A hidden meaning is drawn above her head, and she feels that it's strange and evil.

Suddenly she realizes she's all alone in a dead world, alone with the pain and the stars who want to do bad.

Then she remembers something, the most important

thing in the world, more important than the stars and their secret thoughts, more important than her wandering and her pain: Grandma. Of course she's here looking for Grandma, Grandma's worried for her.

So that was the purpose of the wandering and the pain—Grandma. Her steps gain purpose and she starts running towards her goal, home to Grandma.

But where's home? She can't remember. She's lost her home somewhere in the dark.

Leena despairs.

"Soon, soon, or something terrible will happen . . . I must find Grandma soon!"

The words burn like hot rocks in her mouth, and the pain pushes her on blindly. Blindly, haphazardly, she runs through the dark streets whose names she can't remember. She's wandered through them often before, and still she feels like she's now seeing them for the first time. They too now have some purpose that she doesn't understand. They draw lines and patterns just like the stars, awfully clear patterns, but they have a different intent from her, and that's why it's hateful and evil. They sketch their obscure marks on her path, make crosses, bends, mazes, funnels, set up traps, suck her into their vaults, confuse and disorient her. They want to lead her astray, want her to never find her way home.

No matter where she goes, she goes the wrong way, always wrong. Everywhere's wrong, wrong's been put everywhere, there's no right way. Nothing's right. The town is a horrible optical illusion, and she can't find . . . can't find . . . home.

Yet she walks and walks, goes wrong, wrong, blindly, walks all night. Finally, when she's too tired to be desperate anymore, she falls asleep on her feet, but even in sleep she goes on, goes on out of sheer habit, like the dead, and without a purpose of her own.

WHEN SHE FINALLY COMES to, it's light, bright as day. A narrow, stony street starts at her feet and stretches out beautifully like a long, long ruler, until it reaches the vanishing point and the sky. The old houses tilt on both sides, groggy and stubbornly taciturn, and their dreams are happily unconscious, as they look like they haven't been lived in for a hundred years.

The view feels familiar. The sky made of glass and the street formed of clay . . . Or of porcelain. Old, broken porcelain. This could be her street.

When she then notices the sorrel in the middle of the street, between the stone and the rail, she knows she's come home, knows she's not lost after all. She squats to pick the sorrel, and then—then a rock flutters away from under her palm and starts twittering madly.

Miracle—it's a miracle. She has caused a miracle, made a stone turn into a bird. She clearly felt how the stone moved and flew away from under her hand. And now the bird was singing, a more heavenly song than any bird before.

Leena is happy as can be, weary and tired from walking so long. She's been given the stone and the music, and the sorrel is guiding her home.

She's treasuring the sorrel on her palm, going where the street takes her. The stone is singing madly on top of her head, Bach is singing in the stone's throat, and Leena knows that she and the sorrel and the song will be there soon.

Odd. First she had lost everything, the music in the water and her home in the dark, and now she's gotten everything back, like a gift, not deserved nor undeserved, now that she's no longer looking for anything. And on top of that, she's been given the stone and the miracle that flew from under her hand. Her hand has woken the stone.

And the pain is gone. The pain has forgotten her and gone away. Only her fingers tingle now. The sorrel? Nettle? Her sorrel was somehow connected to the nettle and the miracle of the stone and bird, but what it was, she couldn't remember, though the miracle sang like crazy above her head.

And it didn't matter—remembering. She feverishly longed to see her grandma, it was the only thing that mattered anymore.

And soon she will see Grandma, soon she'll run into Grandma's arms. Now she's at her gate, almost there.

When she turns into the yard, through the gate, it starts

snowing ashes in front of her. Big, white flakes fall onto her hand and soon melt away. No, no, it's not ash but snow. Odd that she's not cold at all even though she's only wearing a cotton dress. But she's so happy that she doesn't even remember to be cold. And she knows that now she's found her way home she'll never again have to be cold.

Never, never, sings the stone above her head, rising higher and higher up.

Leena feels dizzy. Why . . . why is it so strange—her own yard? What's happened? Nothing. That's just it: nothing. Everything is strangely dead, motionless, and has a feel of being disremembered and forgotten. The feeling of eternity, familiar from the street, abides here, too: her house looks like it hasn't been lived in for a hundred years or ever.

Not ever.

Is Grandma in the window? Leena's heart beats, and the windows stare at her blindly. Why have the windows been covered with paper? Old newspaper yellowed by time and the sun? Leena's frightened and confused.

She looks around her in awe. A few ancient wooden shacks surround the yard, one of them tilted, another kneeling, all fallen into a heap, squatting, as if expecting the end of the world. All of them old acquaintances, and still they have a strange look about them, of empty thoughts and deserted, covered windows.

And in the yard, between the cobblestones worn smooth by stepping feet, grow a hand-tall chamomile, cart-track plant, mint, and other greedy grasses that have conquered the space from human steps. The wormwood by the wall of her house is almost as tall as Leena, and by the back stairs the nettles reach the eaves as if possessed. They grow visibly, you can see and hear them grow, whispering madly. Soon they'll cover everything, everything; conquer, push over, eat out of their way, weave a terrible fortress around and over the yard—like the rose bushes in the enchanted dream that lasted a hundred years.

A hundred years . . . Had it happened? Had she come too late, found her way home too late? Come home a hundred years too late?

The yard's abandoned, the grasses are singing: a hundred years, a hundred years too late, home a hundred years too late.

But the bird, the heavenly miracle, born from stone, is climbing higher and higher, nearing the high heavens, out of its mind declaring:

Make a wish! The spell will break! Make a wish! The spell will break!

But Leena's too tired to wish for anything. The centennial dream of the deserted yard has put a spell on her, and she can't . . . she can't . . . believe anymore . . . in the miracle. She's immensely tired, cold too, and it's snowing in her way. Snow and ashes, dreams and ashes fall softly in her way, and in the snow, in the ashes, in this dream, the miracle is buried, the promise hidden somewhere.

Make a wish! The spell will break! Make a wish! The wisdom will be revealed!

Stone bird. Stone wisdom. It came out of the stone's throat. The bird's.

The bird's cry hurts her strangely, but she's tired and doesn't make a wish. Bound by a vague hope and fear she runs the last bit home. Just a few more steps, and soon she'll be home, just a few little steps and she'll get to go to bed, just a few, and there, the stairs, just a little step and then—

"Grandma!"

Leena stumbles on the stair, slips, and falls on her mouth—falls from the pier into the water.

THEN NOTHING WORTH MENTIONING happened anymore, and what didn't even happen was already abundantly narrated: the stone that had turned into a bird pierced the sky like a pane of glass, the sun exploded and went out, and the hot shards fell into the sea. And even if the quaking of the sky and the earth lasted forever and maybe longer, in a blink of an eye there was silence. There was the dream and the century-old kingdom of dream, bottomless water and the end of the world.

On this side of the end of the world, under the pier, in the oily water the straw-yellow hair spread like a strange flower, glowed in the sun for a while and modestly hid its graces before anyone had time to pick it up. And far out, where the green watery space brightened, the umbrella sailed all alone towards the sky and the sunset, full of wind and its owner's happy dreams.

EEVA-LIISA MANNER (1921–1995) is one of the most celebrated postwar Finnish poets. In addition to fifteen volumes of poetry, she published several volumes of prose and wrote plays for radio and the theater. Her collection *Tämä matka* (This Journey, 1956) is considered a landmark work of Finnish modernism. She was also a translator of English and German literature. Manner received numerous national prizes and awards for her work, including the Aleksis Kivi Prize (1967) and the Finnish State Award for Literature (1961).

TERHI KUUSISTO is a Finnish writer and literary translator. She grew up listening to Eeva-Liisa Manner's voice through her translations of such children's classics as *Alice's Adventures in Wonderland* and *The Little Water Sprite*. It now makes perfect sense to Terhi that *Girl on Heaven's Pier* concerns a girl lost in her imagination, loving and fearing the water.